~~~~~~~~~~~~~~~~~~~~~~~~~

# *THE DOLPHIN PAPERS*

~~~~~~~~~~~~~~~~~~~~~~~~~

# THE DOLPHIN PAPERS

*A novel by*

*Helen Bonner*

*The Dolphin Papers.* A novel by Helen Bonner

StarthistlePress

HBonnerBooks

412 Broadway, Jackson, CA 95642

(209)257-1832

Published by Lulu

Lulu.com

Printed in the United States of America

First edition

Library of Congress Cataloging-in-Publication Data

Bonner, Helen

Dolphin Papers, sci-fi novel of man/dolphin link / Helen Bonner

    p. cm.

    ISBN 978-1-257-58454-3

dolphins-Fiction      dolphin girl – Sci-fi      evolution - Fiction

*This book is dedicated to my family and to all people everywhere who love animals, dogs, cats, horses, goats, monkeys, even dolphins, and are willing to learn what they have to teach us.*

*Helen Bonner*

*Also by Helen Bonner*

*The Laid Daughter* *a True Story*

*First Love Last* *a Memoir*

*Cry Dance* *a Novel*

# CONTENTS

# *PART 1*

## *GENESIS*

# 1

~~~~~ **GENESIS** ~~~~~

Hard rains off the Pacific Ocean lashed the hills north of San Diego, drove into cracked stucco walls of the isolated marine laboratory, and streamed in rivulets down the tarnished copper spokes of a soaring Spanish dome. A black van slowed in the roadway, paused for a few seconds, then raced away.

Inside the cluttered lab, Dr. Al Waller, once a famous marine biologist, was mixing a protein-shrimp compound for a dyspeptic octopus when he heard a pathetic, haunting cry.

"*Ayudame!*" Help me.

Was it the wind, or his imagination? No one dared pass the *Keep Out* signs down by the gate. He went on feeding Octo. The animal wrapped its tentacles around his wrist and raised its huge head out of the water. Waller admired Octo. The most highly developed of the invertebrates, he housed a well-developed brain in that ugly cartilaginous case. "We're a pair, old boy," he chuckled, drying his hands on the front of his well-filled lab coat. "You're all head and I'm all body."

The cry came again. "*Ayudame!*"

No mistaking it this time. A high voice. Teenaged boy probably, another skinny hope-filled Mexican wetback, risking his life to be an underpaid busboy in some Los Angeles nightspot. They straggled across the border continually. He'd not get involved. Let the Border Patrol do their work.

Maybe it was the old horse someone kept in the pasture by the driveway.

The wind paused for a breather. In the silence, he stopped and listened. Nothing. *Did he leave? Die? Or was someone still out there?*

In a neighboring tank, the coelacanth, half fish, half land creature, crawled ponderously out of the water on rotating pelvic fins, pushing itself along a shelf of rock with paddle-like pectoral fins. "Old Father Fish." Waller ran his finger along the glass. "The first to crawl from the sea." Rare, valuable, the coelacanth was the closest living relative to the prehistoric fishes that gave rise to amphibians and began the chain of animals that led to humans. "And we're not through evolving yet, no matter what they say."

Again the cry, trailing off. "*Ayudame...*" Whoever was out in that downpour was not going away.

Sighing, he hunched his shoulders against the rain and shambled across the central patio into the *sala*, the old resort's once-grand entrance, now a storeroom for unpacked boxes stacked on the heavy, hand-carved chairs. He'd long since given up thinking he would unpack them one of these days.

After surviving years of faculty wars at the university, he'd decided to go independent, do his own research, free of red tape. But the place swallowed money -- first the renovations, then animals needing constant care. The two bottle-nosed dolphins that cost him thousands had not only produced no living young, but last month the female had died, leaving Sonysender, her mate, forlorn and listless. Sony hadn't eaten for days.

By the dim light of the wrought-iron chandelier, he rummaged about in sagging cardboard boxes of hoses, pump parts and scientific journals until he finally found a rain slicker and a flashlight. Coming across his old target pistol, he sighted it at the wrought-iron ceiling fixture, hoping he wouldn't have to use it. The gun was probably unloaded anyway, but he tucked it under his belt. Threats were usually enough.

In the arched stucco doorway, he turned on the floodlights and peered out. Brilliant light shone on the potholed asphalt parking lot, slick and empty. On top of the cracked adobe walls, shards of embedded glass sparkled, keeping out the bravest prowler. Past the flowering bougainvillea that threatened always to reclaim the building, the broken-down tanker truck sank on one flat tire like a dismal penitent before an empty saint-niche in the wall.

No one in sight. Not even the old horse that sometimes grazed by the fence. Pulling his slicker tight, he stepped out into the rain. Cold rivulets streamed down his collar, soaking his undershirt. "Damn!"

He threw the flashlight beam under the giant eucalyptus, its bark forever peeling like torn skin. Nothing. No one behind the truck, either. But as he swung the light under the truck, he saw something hardly discernible from a pile of old clothing.

Waller stepped back. Someone there? Why hadn't the wretch crawled into the cab, out of the wind and rain? Was this a set up for a robbery? He snorted aloud. What a disappointment that would be -- a water-smeared checkbook, often in the red, a lonely cetacean, and a sick cephalopod.

He circled at a safe distance, shouting the only Spanish that came to him. *"Avanzarle."* Come forward. Even when he swung the powerful beam under the truck, the figure remained a sodden, silent, mass, motionless.

"Damn!" Groaning, Waller got to his knees and peered under the low, greasy engine.

Light fell on a delicate, smooth, young face partially hidden in mud-matted strings of long black hair. A woman! Blood oozed from a deep gash on the side of her head, and one cheek was scraped raw. Even in the bright glare, she didn't open her eyes.

Waller stood up, arching his back to ease the pain, and glared at the heavens. "Damn!"

Dropping to his knees again, he crawled into the tight, oily space and pushed his slicker under her limp body. Backing out, he got a firm hold and dragged her out feet first, cringing as her head bumped against the pavement, but he had no choice.

One hand easing his back, he shone the light across the still figure sprawled face up in the rain. He noted the cheap nylon dress, torn in places, and over that, a man's athletic jacket. Her high-heeled shoes, cracked patent leather, seemed ridiculous, pathetic, but somehow touching.

Everything about her said *Made in Mexico*, in every sense of the word. Coyotes, wretched men who took money to get desperate people across the Mexican border, sometimes shoved them out of vans on these lonely back roads. From the look of her lacerations, this son of a shark had not even slowed down. People. Their treachery against one another was like no other species.

He scanned the shadows, the shabby eucalyptus trees beyond the drive, half hoping someone would materialize to take her off his hands. No such luck. The rain came harder, beating on the tiled roof, pouring over the clogged drains. He had to get her inside.

"Something tells me I'm going to hate myself for this." Getting his arms under her, he stumbled awkwardly and nearly dropped her, the vertebrae at the base of his spine sending sparks of pain. He had to brace his back against the truck before he could get moving a second time, and then he lunged through the gate crabwise, using her feet to push the gate open. Breathing hard, he heaved her onto the long wooden bench in the *sala*. She groaned. "Sorry," he said, "But I didn't exactly invite you."

Her eyes remained closed. Her hair smelled like muddy fur. In the glare of the one dangling light bulb, she looked pale and very young. Seventeen? Eighteen? She had the perfect classic features of so many Mexican women, sculpted wing-like eyebrows over a straight, narrow nose, delicate high cheekbones.

Neither beautiful nor unbeautiful right now, just a problem he didn't want or need.

Always happier with marine animals than with people, he certainly didn't want to nursemaid this one. "I'm no Florence Nightingale," he growled. Her eyes remained closed. He'd get her out of here as fast as he could. Let the Border Patrol take over.

Ducking through the double doors that swung into the laboratory, he grabbed a towel from the pile next to the cluttered examination table, and hurrying back, wiped the girl's tangled hair away from the wound. Looked bad. The cut was deep, blood already clotting. He examined abrasions on her legs, arms and hips. Bad.

Her dark skin was blue under the eyes. She felt as cold and clammy as one of his fish. Pulling off the wet dress, he rubbed the towel briskly under her blue-veined breasts, across her wide hips and rounded belly. She stiffened. Her eyelids fluttered.

"Don't worry, lady. This might be some man's fantasy, undressing a mysterious young senorita in the midnight hours, but I could do nicely without whatever soap opera you've gotten me into." He wrapped her in a fishy-smelling blanket from his bed.

Hypothermia, probably. Extreme exposure. Shock. Probably internal injuries as well. This was more serious than he was prepared to handle.

In the lab, he searched for the phone by the fish tank's yellow light, found it under heaps of papers, then got only a buzz of brittle static. "Damn!" The phone never worked when it rained. And the truck had a flat, dammit. To get help, he would have to walk all the way to the gas station, at least a mile, and a steep uphill climb returning. The rain would make it worse. Could she survive the wait?

In the old commercial kitchen, rummaging around the fish-smelling sink and the ancient black stove smelling of grease, he found a bottle of Scotch and poured a jigger to prepare himself for a rainy hike. *Ah. That's better.* It warmed him like a mother's hug. Not that his mother ever hugged him, blue stocking intellectual that she had been.

He took another jigger to his patient, and lifting her head, tipped a dose between her parted lips. She writhed, coughing. Her eyes fluttered open. "Jesus! Maria!" Her cry held such pain that Al was glad he'd left medicine decades ago.

"What happened?" he asked. "*Que pasa?*"

Her attempts to talk came in weak gasps and moans. "*Coyotes ... pagar ... frontera ...*" He understood only a little Spanish, but he understood that much. Smugglers had taken her money then dumped her on the road, probably leaving her for dead. Who knows how far she had crawled to get shelter under the truck?

He put on the muddy slicker. "I'm going for help," he said, more to himself than to her. As he headed for the door she reached out, got hold of the edge of the slicker, and held on. Her eyes met his with a desperate gaze. "Save my baby," she begged. Spoken perfectly.

In what soap opera had she learned that one, he wondered?

"Save your baby! Lady, you've come to the wrong kind of doctor."

"Ah. Doctor. Medico." A sigh of relief. Her head fell back. Her small vulnerable face was already closing, her lips bluish around the edges. He watched helplessly as the light in her eyes dimmed, the lamp of her young life receding further and further into darkness. Her fingers loosed their hold on his slicker.

He thought then of the soft rise of her belly. He got the stethoscope and shoved it under the blanket. Yes, the beating of a tiny heart. And distinctly under his palm came the quick demanding thrust of life, a small heel already kicking out against the disastrous malfunction of its life support system.

He leaned against the wall, stunned. Here he was, nothing but ocean on one side and miles of eucalyptus on the other, and this baby comes to him. To him! Uncanny. Perhaps there was such a thing as fate. No. Ridiculous.

What if he *could* save her baby? How far along? Any hope? A caesarean? What then? There were laws against that kind of thing. He'd dropped out of med school years ago.

No time to think about it. She was no longer breathing. He had about five minutes before a second life would be lost. Pulling off the slicker and heaving the still warm body into his arms, he pushed through the swinging double doors, laid his burden on the surgical table and rolled up the sleeves of his fishy lab coat.

The air of the laboratory was thick with primal odors -- salt, seaweed, fish, mold. Octo, he noted, was responding well to his ministrations. His tentacles hungrily explored the mossy glass of the aquarium. Waller thought it a rather good sign.

# 2

## ~~~~~ CREATION ~~~~~

A messy, bloody job. Waller had to keep well in mind his first lesson in scientific objectivity. His high-school teacher had pulled a live frog out of a tank, pushed its long, girlish legs down on the dissecting table. "The first true land vertebrates, 400 million years ago," he'd said briskly, while cutting away flesh to disclose a still beating heart.

How perfect was the tiny fetus Waller now held in his gloved palm. No bigger than a child's fist. Undoubtedly premature. Its eyelids were still fused shut, but complete, as were the fingernails. He traced tiny vestiges of gill pouches on each side of its rather square head. All early embryos resemble each other anatomically, he knew. Embryos of birds have gill slits, and sometimes closely related species, such as dolphin and human. Still, he found the resemblance to dolphins fascinating.

Insane, he told himself. *Insane to think I can do this.* And why not? he told himself. Other species develop outside the womb, in eggs, for example. Years ago, he'd taken an ordinary glass water tank and cobbled it together for a newborn dolphin with an infection. Thanks to all the lab equipment he'd salvaged from the university, it had worked. Now if he could just transfer the inert but still-breathing handful of flesh from the dead mother to the sterilized tank.

He did it, moved the fetus from its mother's womb to a seawater womb of glass, and there it floated, ragged and seemingly lifeless, like something in a Chinese pickling shop.

But this was no dolphin. It would not be easy to replace nature's simple and efficient umbilical cord, which not only delivered oxygen and nutrients to the infant, but removed waste products from the blood. Feverishly, he worked on adaptations until, again and again, he fell asleep at the table, medical books and lab records open, electroencephalograph and stethoscope at his fingertips, while the tiny creature floated in the water tank, ghostlike companion in the long night hours.

The storm moved on without his noticing. Hours turned into days. In the cluttered lab, he lived on caffeine, potato chips and packaged doughnuts.

Just when he thought he'd solved one problem, another would crop up. Amniotic fluids, normally expelled during labor, encouraged bacteria. He used antibiotics until he feared they were no longer effective, then looked up ancient herbal remedies to build its immune system.

He kept a meticulous log, an hourly record of his progress, so he could someday show the world how he'd done it. If it lived.

Days later the small life seemed to have stabilized. It floated peacefully in the glass tank, breathing regularly, tubes running from every orifice. He'd done it!

He felt as if his whole life, including his early years in med school, had gone the way it had just to prepare him for this challenge. Exhilarated, high on success and adrenalin, he poured himself a Scotch and raised a toast. "Here's to fate, and here's to science!"

As he was congratulating himself, he heard a car out on the front road. Was there still a world out there? He'd almost forgotten. Opening a shutter, he peered out. Headlights approaching the lab. He slammed it shut. No one had any business on his road. People in town considered him a loony, and he rather liked it that way.

Could it be someone looking for the missing woman? He glanced at the body lying on the surgical table, wrapped in a black plastic sheet. There'd been no time to do more.

He locked all the doors, turned out all the lights, then rushed outside to lock the gates. The car was not even hesitating at the *keep out* signs. What if it was the police? What if they had a search warrant?

Back inside, he scooped up the body, starting to smell, carried it out the back door, and laid it in the shallow, dry drainage ditch. He had shoveled only a few scattered inches of sandy dirt over the top when he heard someone rapping on the front gate. In the darkness he crouched, silent, motionless, heart thumping like a great hammer in his chest, until he heard the car circle and go back toward the highway.

On fear-weakened legs, he crept to the gate, where he found a Jehovah's Witness flier stuffed between the boards. The pamphlet threatened the doom of Armageddon, but offered resurrection of the body. Laughing with relief, he patted the round belly under his bloody lab coat. "Why would anyone want to keep this body?" The tired old horse nickered from the weedy pasture.

Behind the lab, he shoveled a little more dirt over the woman's body and piled a few rocks on top to keep animals away. Good enough for now. It had already taken too long.

Hastening back inside, he found the tiny creature turning blue, its heartbeat dangerously slow. Desperate, he took it out of the tank and cut two fine slits where the gills would be and forced oxygen into the minuscule lungs. Not only did the miniature heart keep beating, but he hoped the pumped air would slowly force the lungs to expand, making the heart even stronger.

Anxiously he watched over the infant until once again it floated peacefully in the glass womb, its color a healthy, rosy red.

Pouring a drink, he raised a toast, remembering the introduction to the graduate dissertation he had written years ago. *A human fetus, living in a saline solution, the ocean of its mother's womb, resembles the fetus of sea mammals, like dolphins.* He had proposed that *Hydra Humans, humans adapted to the sea from the time of birth, could lead to our survival on this troubled planet.* He could still hear the mocking laughter of his professors when they rejected his thesis. "Sure, Waller. How are you going to test that theory? Send out a lab order for a living fetus? Knock up some girl?"

He had achieved considerable success, though, publishing a popular book before he was thirty -- *Hydra Humans - Evolution as reflected in the Dolphin* -- proving dolphins had once been land animals before they returned to the sea, and suggesting that we could return to the sea as well. His book even claimed the possible superiority of the dolphin, *considering the eternal inter-species warfare of humans.*

That brought some backlash, of course, so he'd dropped his hydra-human hypothesis in favor of something more practical -- what we could learn from the evolution, language, and behavior of dolphins. He'd bought this broken down resort with his book profits, a modest inheritance, and a couple of grants, put a pair of dolphins in the giant pool, and set about trying to prove that they might have something to teach us, if we would only enter their lives on their terms, instead of insisting they come into ours on our terms.

Now, fate or accident, there it was in front of him, a miniature hydra-human floating in a glass water tank! Imagine the headlines: *Scientist saves baby in seawater womb. Hydra humans ahead?* Talk shows would feature him. Maybe even a movie. He poured another congratulatory drink.

It was time to turn things over to the proper authorities. Rummaging for the phone, he paused, receiver in hand. And who might that be? 911? EMT's certainly wouldn't know what to do with it. The Border Patrol? No way! The hospital? He knew something about that world. Would any of those scalpel jockeys know how to keep it alive? Who then?

The police? Murder would be a cop's first thought if he found the mother's mutilated body in a shallow grave behind the lab. And they'd say worse when they saw what he'd put in a jar. They'd say he killed the mother so he could take the baby for his experiments. A mad doctor. A *Frankenstein*.

Slamming the phone down, he sat at his desk, staring into darkness, until head on his arms, he fell into an exhausted, alcoholic sleep, bubbling tanks and the hum of pumps merging with dreams and memories. Pieces of his old doctoral dissertation surfaced like flotsam and jetsam -- *A human fetus, the closest living equivalent to sea mammals, lives in an underwater world... Sea-adapted humans could lead to our survival on this troubled planet* -- the words were drowned out by nightmarish laughter as he forced himself awake.

He still believed in those college-boy theories. He argued them still when a rare invitation came to speak. *We all came from the sea. Dolphins were once land animals, walking around on two feet like we do, but they went back. No one knows why. Most likely because survival was easier there. Might it not be possible now to return to the sea? Could we not, with deliberate mutations, readapt to the sea, especially since we are making such a mess of things on land?* That always brought ironic laughter.

*Maybe dolphins made a smart move, going back to the sea. Maybe they are actually the higher evolutionary species, smarter than we are. After all, they have no need for houses or cars or clothes or any of the claptrap humans work so hard for. Nor do they blow each other up in endless wars.*

He stood up and circled the lab. Yes, he still believed. Evolution led to the arrogant human species, but surely it did not end there. "Heaven forbid we give up our cherished position as the ultimate creation," he said to the swellfish, who only pressed his round red mouth against the glass like a kiss. The coelacanth stared at him from ancient scaly eyes.

Nearby, the tiny fetus -- would they call it a baby? -- floated serenely in the glass womb, moving like seaweed in the flow of water pumping in and out. If he picked up the phone, what about that tiny life, so fragile? If he told the world, it would become no more than a freak, passed around from bureaucrat to scientist and back until it died. After all he'd done, he couldn't bear the thought.

Slowly the shattering realization came. He could never, *never* under any circumstances, tell anyone! It would mean death for the infant, and prison or worse for him. He dropped again into his desk chair, head in hands. "My god, what have I done?"

From a nest of lazily floating tentacles, the octopus raised its enormous, boneless head, seeming to mock him with its white depthless eye.

All night he paced the floor, arguing back and forth. If he called the authorities now, wouldn't he be seen as heroic? The dying woman had begged him to save her child, and he -- a marine biologist -- had done so. His hands went again to the phone. *Call now while you still can.* But he had waited too long. There were sure to be charges brought against him: he'd murdered a woman and experimented on a baby.

*Face it. Call.*

And watch the infant die in the hands of others? No, he could not do that.

Sometime before dawn, stumbling to the kitchen, he poured a cup of black coffee and found a stale donut. With shaking hands, he drank the bitter black brew. What was he thinking? If he continued this ... this ... insane experiment, he would make himself an outlaw for the rest of his life. Even if the creature lived, even if it eventually achieved some kind of normalcy, he could *never never never* disclose what he had done.

Wait. There was another option. A dark option. If he hadn't interfered, death would have been the fate of both mother and child anyway. If he himself let it die, no one would ever know what happened here. If his life was ever to be his own again, that was the only rational answer.

Ready to disconnect the oxygen system, he stood watching the tiny being, its arms and legs swaying with the circulating water, rhythmic as a fish, its heart beating, patient, enduring.

In a nearby tank, the angelfish, strikingly feminine in its airy pink finery, sailed serenely, unaware of the stonefish lying below like a rock in the sand. In an instant, the delicate creature disappeared in a flurry of sand and water, and the rockfish was a rock again.

*Well, that's life,* Waller said aloud, reaching to pull tubes and hoses loose. But he could not make his hands do it.

Later. Let it live for now.

# 3

~~~~~ SONY ~~~~~

The animals had been neglected for days. Octo, without Waller's ministrations, was clearly angry, spitting water, pulling the plug from the aquarium with a wrapped tentacle, disgorging streaks of poisonous purple-black ink.

The lab needed cleaning, too, and marketing -- fresh fish, dolphin food, bought and refrigerated. Most important, Sonar Sender needed attention. Already suffering from the loss of his mate, Sony, a social animal, had grown further depressed.

With two buckets of smelt, Waller pushed through the heavy wooden doors that guarded the pool. On the shallow end, huge boulders formed an island cove where a magnificent brass mermaid knelt, arms outstretched, gazing over the water. But she too had suffered neglect. Streaks of green ran down her round cheeks and adolescent breasts, disappearing into weeds that grew around her thighs.

The dome over the pool was clouded with sediment, green rivulets running from copper spokes that held the once dramatic structure in place. Overgrown palms, avocado and orange trees further screened out light. Once a make-believe Eden, the weedy grounds below were littered with feeding buckets, hoses, nets, dolphin toys, and huge rubber slings, dolphin carriers. The water in the pool was murky but before he could bring up fresh sea- water, the tanker had to be repaired.

Sony was lying in the island lagoon, his three-hundred-pound body drying in the shallows, his duck-like bill resting on the shore. Waller whistled the three notes that always signaled playtime, but as if to punish him for his neglect, Sony did not respond.

When Waller set the feed buckets down, though, the dolphin swam to his feet and rolled over, presenting his soft belly to be stroked. Waller knelt and rubbed him hard, continually amazed by the dolphin's soft skin. Although he looked rubbery as an inner tube, his skin felt more like rose petals, and was so delicate even a torn fingernail could leave a wound. Despite his recent neglect, Sony's skin looked healthy.

Waller tossed a few smelt, landing with a splash just past Sony's flukes, but normally playful, the dolphin only lifted his head and moved into deeper water. Before losing his mate, the dolphin would have slapped his huge flukes flat on the surface, dousing Waller thoroughly, his favorite joke. Now he only squawked once, rather mournfully, and drifted back to his cove, clearly depressed, even though his smile-shaped bill seemed to say otherwise.

The two dolphins had been a joy, exchanging thousands of signals with one another, which Waller had recorded. They had easily learned and responded to more than a hundred of Waller's signed cues.

They cavorted endlessly, clicking, clacking and whistling. They loved music. One morning, he had played a recorded waltz through the pool speakers, awkwardly demonstrating the dance himself, counting *one-to-three* as he twirled on the edge of the pool.

Watching closely, the two dolphins clicked and clacked and whistled gleefully, paused as if conferring, then diving deep, they drove their eight-foot bodies straight up out of the water, ad-libbing their own hilarious dance, walking flipper to flipper, their powerful flukes barely touching the surface, eyes sparkling with mischief, mimicking him as only dolphins can.

No wonder Sony grieved his lost mate. Waller feared he might lose him too, if he didn't do something soon. "You're about to get a companion, Sony," he called.

He trembled at the risk he was taking, but he couldn't keep a growing infant in a crowded glass womb.

Though dolphins, male or female, took good care of their own and were known for their gentleness, there was no way to know how Sony would respond to a human infant. Even human children or family pets, jealous of a newborn, sometimes tried to hurt them. Dolphins could destroy a shark, ramming it in the gut with their hard bills. They had teeth that could rip off an arm, but no bottle-nosed dolphin had ever been known to harm a human being. In fact, there were many legends of dolphins rescuing sailors, and Sony was the best of his kind. Still, he could swallow a baby in one gulp.

Wading into the shallow end of the pool, Waller checked the aquatic crib he had built on the island, a rounded, womb-like cove, half in and half out of the water, lined with silky-smooth rubber.

Above a floating mat shaped like a lily pad, a flotation device held a baby bottle just above water.

One last time, he checked the heating and purification systems. The dolphin, roused from his torpor by curiosity, pushed his bill against Waller's hands as he made adjustments. "You be good now," he scolded.

Convinced all was in readiness, he straightened his shoulders and stepped into the lab, which looked like a set from an old *Frankenstein* film, the metal table still stained with the mother's blood, the floor cluttered with discarded tubes, surgical instruments, and oxygen tanks. The infant -- he had to admit it was no longer a fetus -- floated in serene innocence in its glass womb, fed by tubes, sucking her thumb in peaceful aquatic innocence. After weeks in a water womb, she weighed just four pounds, no bigger than a plucked chicken.

Yes, *she*. She was clearly female. Her skin was blue white, with shades of violet around the smooth genitals. Her lashless eyes, still closed most of the time, were softened by violet hollows, and her thin lips, even the gill-like scars on her neck, were a soft mauve. So far, she was hairless.

Some would think her strange looking, but she had her own kind of beauty, he thought, somewhat like a sea anemone.

She. It was time to give her a name. Why had he not done that sooner? Would a name have given her an identity? A name bestows personal distinction, which he had been reluctant to do. Without a name was she only an animal, and he ethically free to control her life? Now, about to be born, she deserved a name.

Watching the tiny creature move in rhythm with the water, coming and going, he decided on Mara -- in French, *la mer,* for the sea. In Spanish, her mother's language, *la mar.*

Hands shaking with trepidation and excitement, he disconnected all the tubes and lifted her from the tank. "Happy Birth Day, Mara."

Her eyes flew open. She wailed, staring into his eyes as if he were a monster. Her tiny limbs flew out in panic, flailing in fury at being born into open and frightening space.

"Good," he said, "A healthy howl is just what those lungs need." In cupped hands, he carried her to the pool and waded in, water up to the armpits of his lab coat. As he lowered her, still squalling, into the heated water, she relaxed, no doubt feeling its familiar support, and there she rested, rocked by water, cradled by the lily pad.

Sony, always the curious one, eased his rubbery bulk from the depths and surfaced nearby. Circling close, he nudged Waller's hands away from the floating crib. "No, Sony, she is not food."

The dolphin lifted his great head, opened his jaws wide, and protested, "Mo-mo-mo," a fine spray burbling from his blowhole. Teasing, he nudged the baby with his beak, eyes shining with mischief.

"She is not a toy either," Waller said, lifting her out of the water. Again the tiny arms and legs flailed frantically, the overhead dome echoing her cries until he put her back in the glass tank.

The next day, Waller again carried her to the rock island and laid her in the cove cradle while Sony hovered close by. When she continued to cry, chest heaving as if every gulp of air were painful, Sony was distressed. He flung himself upward, strutting on his flukes to get a better look, falling with a splash that nearly washed her out of the crib, then raced around her in huge wave-building circles, challenging her to play. Waller was convinced the dolphin knew this was a creature like himself, and wanted very much to befriend her.

Repeatedly Waller tried to get her to take the nipple of the suspended bottle, but accustomed to being fed intravenously, she would not take it, would not suck, but turned her head away. He tried putting syrup on the nipple, tried thrusting milk-drenched fingers into her mouth, but she only lay still and silent, as if she had no will to live.

Sony pushed his favorite toy, a red floater with bells attached, directly at her, waiting expectantly. He brought morsels of shrimp and sardines from his food bucket until the water was murky with debris.

Cold, wet, and discouraged, Waller moved away. Sony moved in and there he floated for hours, stroking her with his flippers, nuzzling her with tender watery grunts. Finally the dolphin shoved the suspended bottle toward her -- was it an accident? -- her blue-white cheeks drew in, and she began to suck. There Sony stayed, huge flukes curving over her like angel wings.

The following day, the dolphin leaped to life, whipping around the pool in puppyish delight as soon as Waller carried the infant through the wooden gates. When he placed her in the crib, Sony came racing up with pleased grunts, barks and clicks, nudged her again and again toward the bottle, and soon she was nuzzling her small pale mouth against it.

From a nearby bench, Waller watched with hope and pleasure. Hour after hour, the dolphin hovered near, persistently nudging, stroking, burbling and rocking, then whipping around the pool, nearly engulfing her in his wake.

Losing his mate might be why Sony took such a mothering interest in the infant. Sony tended Mara with inexhaustible good humor, total devotion, and never-failing vigilance. He hovered nearby while she slept, eager for her to wake. He carried her to deep water, let her sink, paddle, and surface on her own, before lifting her gently in his great jaws and taking her back to the crib.

Since Waller knew nothing of babies, he decided to take full advantage of Sony's instincts and the inborn urge of all newborns to imitate the first mothering presence. He stayed away at feeding time and left it to Sony, while he cleaned up the grounds and tended the other animals, always keeping a distant eye on Mara.

Days passed without problems, giving him time to write the monthly grant report, already late. He had promised the Foundation a communication link between humans and dolphins based not on the assumption of human superiority, but on the assumption of dolphin superiority, or at least equality. But how little interest he had for that now when there was so much more he could say -- if he dared.

He had here a human being raised by a dolphin. Such symbiosis was unknown. This water child could become the first actual living bridge between dolphin and human. But he dare not tell them that.

Pushing the forms aside, he unlocked the bottom desk drawer and lifted out the logbook, meticulously maintained day by day, sometimes hour by hour, the record of every minute detail of her existence, exact measurements, formulas, water temperature, schedules, as well as his personal observations. He lay the log on the desk and stroked the water-stained green leather cover. He had made some significant contributions to marine biology before he left the university, but the logbook was the most important work of his life. After his death, it would be his legacy.

Opening the log, he wrote the latest entry in his most careful precise hand, in French. He wrote in French, his second language, to guard against the possibility of snoopers, but also in tribute to Dr. Jean-Marc Itard, the French scientist who, a century ago, had found a wild nine-year-old boy raised by a wolf pack. The boy ran on all fours, killed rabbits with his teeth, and howled at every full moon. Even after working with the boy for years, Itard had been unable to remove the wolf traits and return the boy to human society. That did not bode well for Mara, Waller realized.

*But that was then, this is now*, he reassured himself.

~ ~ ~ ~

In a few weeks, Mara was leaving the cove on her own, Sony swimming under her, thrusting her up whenever she needed to breathe, just as he would an infant dolphin. She followed Sony everywhere, reached out her arms for him when her eyes first opened, cried for him when Waller carried her inside for safety or medications.

He did not find it difficult to keep his distance. He had never liked babies. He certainly had no memory of being a bundle of joy to his own middle aged parents, as intellectually aloof as they were, with everything already set in their lives.

One evening he was working in the lab when he heard Sony's piercing shrieks and frantic clacks. Rushing to the pool, he found the baby floating face down by her water crib, unable to right herself. Sony dropped under her, pushed her to the surface, then brought her to Waller, holding her gently in his duck-like bill. She might have drowned if it were not for Sony. No father ever had a better baby sitter.

At three months he wrote: *She is doing well, even gained a pound or two. Because she spends almost all her time in the pool, I have gradually reduced the temperature of the water to avoid bacterial infections and increased the oil and fat content of her formulae to protect her from cold. She's developed a sleek coat of fatty tissue under her skin that operates much like the wetsuits of divers.*

He felt a proud urge to show her to someone, this incredible water child, but there were still too many problems to be solved. He would wait until he had clearly proven the adaptation of a birthed infant to a saline environment, then he would inform the authorities. They would surely see that he had saved the life of the infant and contributed important new knowledge to science and medicine. But not yet.

~ ~ ~ ~

At six months, he wrote: *The chemicals have affected her pituitary gland, which controls growth and coloration. She is still very small, almost hairless, her skin pale, but she has continued to develop her lung capacity, staying under about five minutes to Sony's forty, and is imitating some of his sounds. Sometimes she cries, like any other baby, then Sony barks until I come. No father ever --- Father!* He put the pen aside, closed the log. He was not her father! No father would leave his daughter, even an adopted daughter, to be raised by another animal. No. He must remember he was a scientist, not her father.

He turned back to the first pages of the log, water blotched writing cramped in those places where he had been nearly exhausted those first days. Under the rows of facts and figures, he had written: *Her name is Mara, and she is beautiful.* He smiled to himself. Hardly scientific, but truth is truth.

~ ~ ~ ~

When she was nine months old, he wrote: *Though not much bigger than a baby of six months, she is exceptionally strong. Sony brings her the choicest morsels of his own food, shrimp and sardines, which she scoops up with her mouth as she swims, like he does. The wetsuit effect works. I can fill the pool with seawater without heating it now, so less bacteria. Because she is almost constantly moving, she is not fat, but muscular.*

~ ~ ~ ~

At one year he wrote: *She is still small, but stronger than any child her size, since she swims and plays with Sony for hours. She grows ever stronger on fish, sea plants, and formulas rich with oil. She does not scoop food up with her mouth anymore, but uses her hands, and sometimes a cup. But my attempts to teach her to talk, to imitate me, seem meaningless to her. Attempts to keep her out of the water, to get her to walk, have been disastrous. If she is out longer than a few minutes, especially if she gets dry, she squeals and squirms with discomfort, and looks at me as if I am some kind of monster.*

He shuddered, remembering that he had dropped her yesterday, carrying her from the pool, squirming and slippery. Fortunately, she landed on soft grass, but before he could get to her, she'd crawled, scurried across concrete, getting back to Sony. Her skin, toughened by salt but still delicately thin, was badly torn.

*Now she is ever more reluctant to let me near.*

He reminded himself that the child's fear of him had its advantages. Socialized with a dolphin, everything she knew had to come from Sony, his language, perhaps even his thoughts.

Wasn't that what he wanted when it all started?

~ ~ ~ ~

# 4

## ~~~~~ MARA ~~~~~

When Mara was two, Waller sat at the poolside with his logbook, watching them play. Riding on Sony's sleek body, she thrust herself clear out of the water, tossed the ball into the net, and disappeared under the waves, sleek as a sailfish. When Sony reemerged with the ball, she chased him, wrestling it out of his huge teeth, the two making clacking and creaking sounds obviously meaningful to each other, though not to him. She laughed, that most human of sounds gurgling up from her belly. Her eyes were as bright as the dolphin's, a brightness he had never seen in humans.

Though still nearly hairless, her rose-shadowed skin still pale, she was a beautiful child, exceedingly graceful, he thought, as she dove into the water. Her feet, adapted by constant swimming, were long and slender, the heels disappearing into the ankle, toes pointing down and outward, like a ballet dancer's.

She had a sense of fun. She mimicked Sony, rushing up from the water, powerful legs kicking so fast she appeared to stand on the surface for a split second before Sony chased her to the other side of the island. Her happy laughter spilled like a waterfall, like the water in which she lived and breathed.

~~~~

Mara crows with delight as a globe of brilliant red lands in the water. White froth leaps, curling around the dancing ball, the sun careening off its red wetness. Water, tile, domed sky, all reflect a rosy glow.

A winged creature hovers above the surface of the pool, its translucent wings dazzling. Mara sees a great cross-wiring of wing muscles whirring like blades, filling her ears with their buzz. Floating motionless beside it, she watches. Bombed by a drop of water, the fragile body is dragged onto the water, where it struggles, wire legs waving, wings caught in the water's taut surface.

The struggle stops. A wave carries it, balanced on the crest, sun glinting off its iridescent green-gold eyes. When its golden spirit dims, she sees a flash of energy, a burst of light, then the being leaves. Only a shell remains.

A leaf falls upon the surface of the pool. Mara pushes toward it, curious. The leaf is a profusion of slight pulsating cells, held together and fed by a throbbing red network of veins, like those in her own hand. She feels its greenness and yellowness flowing through her like a great river, spilling from the broken stem.

She plunges to steal the ball from Sony, balances it on the tip of her nose, and becomes the ball, becomes the water, herself the union between them. Faster and faster, the ball spins. She sights the net, and lifting only slightly, allows the ball to float into the hoop.

Sony's great smooth mass pushes up under her, spins her about, the sun whirls through white sky, gleaming in spokes of greenish copper. Her voice spills like water in mindless imitation of the radiant life around her.

She slips down around Sony's wide throat, and grasping his dorsal fin, allows him to pull her through the water like a knife blade. High thin sounds stream from his pulpy blowhole, filling her mind with bursts of color. The wind, whistling through his flippers, creates an effervescence of oxygen. He carries her to the gray-green depths, cool and shady. Above, the surface of the water is a canopy of light, sun dazzled. He turns an easy figure eight, comes to rest against her, and grows quiet. The water stills around them.

Lying beside him, she picks up the images in his mind -- an endless expanse of gray and green, split with streaks of light from high above, where a shifting golden surface divides him from the sky. The vision in his mind intensifies. He leaps beside a great gray hull, pulsing like a thunderstorm through the sea. He leaps again, twirls for joy, and dives into the wake. There he becomes part of a great mass of Sonys, moving together across miles of water, united as if in one thought. All the while he lies there.

She slips back into the depths and floats idly, sunlight swimming in webbed patterns across the walls of the pool. Sony surfaces under her. She lies across his sleek back, feeling the great pulsations of his being. They merge with her own, unifying them, connecting them with everything, water, rock, sky---there is no separation.

Sony surfaces, opens his huge mouth, sharp teeth gleaming. He wants her to stroke his sensitive gums, but she crawls onto the smooth, sun-warmed rocks, watches each drop of water slide off her arms in shiny streams, down a rock worn sleek and black, revealing tiny white stars in granite.

The humid air is rich, thick with smells, the clean sharp scent of Sony, the bittersweet lemon blossoms from the trees by the wall, the bristling odor of shrimp in her feeding tray. Rivulets of saliva stream like honey in her mouth, and her tongue pulses with the lush red-orange flavor of soft shells. She probes the corners of her tray, finds a particle, dips it in water and eats. The flavor fills her mind with images of wiry red legs waving, drawing to themselves minute particles of vegetation.

The rock is drying under her body; her skin tightens on her skull. There is nothing she dislikes so much as being dry, losing her fluidity. She slips off the rock, feels the water close with trembling coolness over her thighs, hips, shoulders, and finally, the top of her head.

Heavy doors open with a metallic grating sound. Sony is immediately at the water's edge, dancing and barking for fish, bright colors of anticipation in the light around him. The dark shadows of the island draw Mara deeper into them, and she lies hidden there, all her radiance withdrawn, condensed in a deep core, as if she is pushed again into a small glass world, knees drawn up, blood lumping and clotting its way through veins fed from a painfully throbbing source. The blurred white shape moves closer, throwing dark shadows. She remembers being lifted, terrified, into the void, unsupported by water, her hands and legs kicking out, frantic.

Sony never fears the dull white being, sends no warning calls. He lays his chin against the being's feet. She hovers near her island, waiting for him to go away, but like a great frog, he sits on his haunches and watches her, not sending and receiving like Sony, but a stare that chills her. Finally, he sighs heavily, groans to his feet, and goes away. She washes the smell of his hands from a shrimp, nibbles at it, and throws it away.

The land being leaves. The terror ebbs. She knows it was, and is not. Little by little, colors return. She sees Sony above, masses of white froth where he jumps and pirouettes in the pleasure of feeding. She takes mouthfuls of bright curled green that taste of grass, fresh and watery. She bites into a round red fruit, exploding sweet juice into her mouth, sending aromas of flowers into her nostrils. She savors the chewy red skin, mushes tiny black seeds into the white sweet pulp.

She throws her head back and plays with a hundred variations of sound. Sony darts under her and leaps. Clinging to the red band around his middle, she rides him round and round, until he shakes her off and seizes her gently in his great teeth, as if to devour her. Instead he tosses her, comes racing under her. She pushes off his speeding body and shoots into the air. Water flies from her in diamond tipped arrows. The sun spins above in a great white bowl. She laughs for joy.

~ ~ ~ ~

Waller wrote in the log: *Two is the age at which the human brain begins to be most amenable to learning languages. By her behavior and by her imitations, I can see she already understands Sony, interprets his sonar soundings, his clicks and clacks, his thousand expressions of fear and joy. Next she must learn to speak human language, to pass on what she learns, to teach us the language of dolphins, perhaps even someday share with us the secrets of a dolphin heart! But . . .*

Waller hesitated, unwilling to put his fears in writing. Mara was well past the age most children learn to talk, and he was concerned. A child locked away from others may survive, if fed and otherwise cared for, but it will not learn language. Mara was not talking in any way a human would understand.

Could vocal chords damaged by early gill experiments and a mouth shaped to whistles and clicks be trained to make the subtle sounds of human language? He was sure she was learning sonar echolocation and other kinds of dolphin communication; she might even be communicating with Sony telepathically, as it sometimes seemed, though he had no way to prove it.

She would have nothing to do with his attempts to teach her to talk. She wouldn't stay still and listen to him, much less repeat his words.

Actually, he had to admit he was making little progress in relating to Mara. She hurt herself yesterday, trying to jump off the mermaid's shoulders into the pool. He had to catch her with the net, which she fought with all her strength, and fasten her in a lab tank before he could doctor her scrapes and make sure her arm wasn't broken. Sony's shrieks and clacks and her responding cries had been painful to hear.

He must seem to her a punishing god, swooping down out of nowhere, carrying her away from Sony and her safe water world for reasons she could not understand -- painful examinations, shots against infections or disease, forced spoonfuls of medicines she hated. He was no mother; his manner with her tended to be abrupt, awkward, and impatient. He would have to do better.

He had to get her walking soon, otherwise she would be doomed to live a short and very constricted life. *Function determines structure,* the basis of evolution. Her feet and legs had been shaped by swimming, not walking. Had the possibility of reversing her water adaptation already passed?

*She shows no interest in learning anything that Sony does not do,* he wrote in the logbook. *If she cannot learn to speak, then my dolphin communication research will be useless to the future of mankind.*

*She has mastered water, now she must adapt to land. The first hydra-human must be able to walk and talk! I have work to do, and quickly.*

He drafted a report for the Foundation. The grants that financed his work would run out soon if he couldn't show the agency sufficient progress. Although he was more than convinced he was on the right track, proving that we could learn to understand dolphin communication, writing reports was ever more difficult without disclosing how he learned what he learned -- from Sony's playmate. It was inter-species communication that kept grant money coming in, yet he couldn't tell them what he knew. Not yet.

Carefully he put the logbook in the bottom drawer of the desk and locked it. *Someday what's in this logbook might astonish the world, but not yet.*

~ ~ ~ ~

She was what? Almost three now? Some three-year-olds could count. He'd tried counting her fingers aloud, counting his fingers aloud, counting the number of shrimp in her dish aloud. She showed no interest.

In a San Diego toy store he found a red plastic clock that rang a bell when turned to the hour. Taking it to the pool and getting Mara's attention, he wound it and counted loudly each time the hands moved an hour and the bell sounded. She only stared blankly at him. Finally frustrated, he threw the toy against the wall, breaking it into pieces. Frightened, she rushed to Sony. He hated to see her clinging to Sony's flukes like a child with its mother. After all, she owed her life to him.

Calming himself, he sat down on a poolside bench and tried to keep in mind that her fearful reactions to him were not personal, merely conditioned responses to painful memories. As those dimmed, he hoped she would fear him less.

Mara rested on her island, small twin to the bronze mermaid. He was reminded of the old Eskimo legend of the Seal Goddess -- *The first seal was created when a girl fell from a boat, and hanging on, threatened to capsize the boat and drown them all. They whacked off her fingers to save themselves.* Seals were probably the source of the old Greek legends, too, he thought, watching the girl slide gracefully into the water, seal-like. Greek sailors often told of sirens, bewitching creatures, part woman, part fish, who lured men to their death on the rocks.

There actually were such things as sirens, but they were only small slime-coated lizard-shaped amphibians, living in mud.

Mara was neither siren nor seal, neither legend nor lizard, but a splendid aquatic human being. With her large lungs, she could stay under water longer than eight minutes now, a world record. Sony could still out-swim her, but because she had hands, she had it all over Sony for things like playing ball. Though still small for nearly three, she was very strong, especially her legs. She could kick like a horse when he took her out of the pool for shots.

He wrote in the log: *Every day she is growing stronger, but harder to manage. Where is this headed? Am I, too, pursuing the call of sirens to certain disaster on the rocks?*

# PART II

~~~~~~~

## STRANGERS IN THE GARDEN

~~~~~~~~~~~~~~~~

# 5

## ~~~~~ COMFORT FOOD ~~~~~

For Sony, it was fish and more fish, buckets and buckets. He never seemed to get enough, but Mara had always been curious about other edibles, though cautious. Even as a baby she would spit out a piece of tough seaweed. All food, even cheese or apples, went into the water bowl before she would eat it. She didn't simply gulp food down, like Sony, but savored it in nibbles.

In a weak moment, he'd once let her beg a cupcake off him. After an initial soaring, diving binge, she'd been sick, her system unable to cope with the syrupy stuff. He should have known. Safer to stay with kelp, fruit, vegetables, eggs, and the fish she loved. He couldn't use it as a reward, though, as he did with Sony. She was too smart for that. She was showing much more interest in unusual, colorful toys.

He bought her a bright red and yellow plastic music box, placed it near the edge of the pool, wound it, and stood back hopefully. At a safe distance, she listened, head cocked, enthralled as it clicked off a simple nursery melody -- *Twinkle Twinkle Little Star* -- imitating the high glassy sounds with her still babyish voice until the spring ran down.

When he knelt to rewind it, she dove under the water, emerging a few feet away, watching him demonstrate how it worked. When the notes again came floating from the red plastic box, she laughed her watery laugh and swam in circles, jumping in arcs of delight. When the music stopped, she came to the edge of the pool, took the toy in her hands and wound it herself, just as she had seen him do. Remarkable! he thought. Or was it? She was, after all, three years old now.

She repeated the whole thing again and again, floating a few feet from the edge of the pool, as thrilled with the tinny music as if it were from heaven. He'd finally found something she loved besides Sony.

He wound the music box and placed it a few feet away from the edge of the pool. *To get it, she's going to have to walk.* Expectantly, he watched.

On hands and knees she crawled across tile and grass, her knees scraped and bleeding as she clutched her colorful prize.

When the music stopped, she looked up at him, reaching for the key. "Come and get it, Mara. Walk!" Instead, she gave a mighty spring, turned in midair, and dove cleanly into the water, surfacing at his feet, still clutching the toy. He gave her the key. How could he not?

That afternoon, entering her weight, metabolism, formulas, and water temperature in the log book, he marveled -- *an amphibious human as happy and intuitive as a dolphin, but with the hands and intelligence and love of music of a human being.*

Once again, his hand went to the phone. He longed to tell the world about her, but he couldn't. Not while he lived. Things had gone too far for that. Eventually, she would be the world's first hydra human! But not yet. First she had to walk and talk.

In the gloomy commercial kitchen, looking for something to eat among the litter of food wrappers and cans, Waller felt an emptiness that wasn't hunger. He supposed some might call it loneliness, though he had always preferred being alone.

Way back when he was a grad student, he was bored with most men, with all their talk of sex and football. Women he liked better, but they paid no attention to him, except for one, a shy and fragile-looking classmate who invited him to her apartment for dinner. He'd kept his guard up, stiffly polite through the meal, covering his shyness. Sure enough, after an uncomfortable evening when neither of them seemed to know what to do, she called him "a cold fish" and showed him to the door.

Smiling now at her appropriate choice of words, he remembered what a good cook she was -- superb cordon bleu, key lime pie to make your mouth water. How sick he was of eating out of cans.

Raising the shutters to get more light, he saw someone coming up the front drive on a bicycle, wire basket fastened to the handlebars.

*My god! Was he getting careless? Had he left the gate open?* He hurried outside. "Hey! Didn't you see those no trespassing signs? *Peligroso!* Danger!"

Few intruders ventured up the isolated road past his signs after he added radiation and biohazard symbols, but those who did were easily run off. He weighed over two hundred pounds, his lab coats were ragged and dirty, his hair, going white, blew long and stringy about his head. But this girl had more courage than he expected from a kid in an embroidered blouse and torn jeans.

Catching her breath from the steep climb, she got off the bike. *"Perdoname, pero la playa,* I mean ... the beach." She leaned the bike on a fence post and stroked the muzzle of the old grey horse. "Next I ride him."

He scowled at her. "You missed the turnoff. Go back down the hill and turn left at the gas station."

She smiled, almost challenging Waller to run her off. "The way to the beach I look for. Only."

Bold enough. Doubtless from a tough barrio on the outskirts of San Diego. A long ride on a bicycle. She was about sixteen, he guessed, and probably had a family waiting in a car down by the gas station, sending their prettiest daughter out to sell something.

"This is private property. Get along now!" He stood blocking the open gate.

"Meester?" That's the way people were. If you were nice to them they wanted more.

She lifted an embroidered cloth off the basket. *"Empanadas."* She held up a round, flaky treat. "Home bake. Myself, Dolores, make them with these own hands."

His nostrils quivered with the smell of warm pastries.

"Try. Only twenty cent. My grandmother receipt."

*"Recipe,"* he corrected. Honey glistened inside the flaky crust.

"First one free, no cost to me," she added as he hesitated.

Well, what harm? He took a bite of the *empanada.* She had put a little surprise in the center, a spoonful of flan, made like they make it only on the other side of the border.

She wrapped three of the rolls in a napkin. He paid her and accepted them with a growled warning. "On your way now."

He watched until the girl and her bicycle were out of sight down the hill, his hands shaking as he fastened the padlock. He had been careless. *She could have been anyone.* Had he been so caught up with the child that he forgot how illegal it all was?

The last time he was in San Diego for supplies, the sales clerk had offered a new aquarium mix, but he'd brushed him off. "No. She wouldn't like that." The man had given him a strange look. He had to be more careful. No one must suspect there was anything in that pool but dolphins.

Behind the lab, he noticed the woman's grave was now a sunken basin. The body was surely decayed past recognition by now, but better to be safe. He leveled it with sandy soil and put the shovel back in the neglected adobe that used to be the caretaker's house.

A week later, the Mexican girl showed up again. Ringing the bell on her bicycle, she stood outside the locked gate. "It's me, Dolorita. I bring melt-the-mouth flan."

"Go away," he shouted from the arched doorway.

She placed a colorful casserole on the gatepost. "I come back for the dish. You pay then."

Flan, his great weakness. And now he owed her money.

The next week here she came again, offering tender pastries with a sweet sauce, a subtle mix of apples and cinnamon. As she counted out his change, her eyes took in the pile of moldy journals by the door, the dirty rags on top, the smelly mop in a rusty bucket.

"By the wait," she said, her smile wide and white against olive skin. "You know somebody need a good keephouser? Strong? Honest?"

"No!" he barked. "Be on your way!"

"I come again," she said, undisturbed. "I bring *manzana*, make with these own hands."

"No!" he shouted, but she was already floating down the road on her bike.

When the girl didn't show up the following week, Waller almost regretted being cross with her. Something about her reminded him of a student of his a long time ago, when he was still teaching. A nice looking young woman from Chile, she had seemed genuinely taken with him. In fact, it was she who pushed for marriage, wanting children, while he remained cautious, puzzled about her attraction to him, certain she was making some kind of mistake. She had moved on. He later found out she had died under an abortionist's dirty knife. Though certain he was not involved, he was horrified and painfully grieved, and never approached a woman again.

He'd almost forgotten the promised apple tarts when Dolores brought them on her bicycle. She uncovered them with a flourish. "*Manzana*," she said with pride. "But to make mouth water, need warm oven."

Well, what harm? She was only an ignorant girl who needed the money. "Just this once," he said, letting her in the house, grumbling. "The camel wants to get his nose in the tent."

Puzzled, she eyed the fish tanks. "Fishes, yes, but no camel I see."

In the lab, a sea of clutter and empty cans surrounded an island of dirty kettles and bowls. She ran a finger across a layer of grease on the big commercial stove, eyed the gut-spattered sink. "I don' see how you stand about in all this. You don' need a keephouser, you need a garbage composer." She was already rolling up her sleeves.

"No! No housekeeper!" Waller was loud and stern.

She looked at him, startled by the vehemence of his response.

"I like to be alone," he added, more moderately.

She laughed as if he were joking. "No one alone."

On her next visit, he let her clean the *sala*. "But you must never, never go in there!" he warned, pointing across the patio to the pool's heavy wooden doors. "Lab animals are expensive. Experiments can be ruined by just a sneeze. Do you understand? *Comprende?*"

"What I care about your fishes?" she said.

She emptied boxes and hauled scientific equipment to the lab, while he sorted newspapers, medical journals and lab reports into piles, handing them to her and snatching them back. "Wait. I haven't read it all yet!"

Soon he let her take on the kitchen. She spent hours cleaning the filthy stove, the crusted oven.

One day he'd been cleaning the pool while she worked and hadn't had breakfast when he came back inside. The sinks were shining and the slime washed off the shelves of the big commercial refrigerator. "Now I make you *huevos rancheros*," she announced. "Okay? Owe me nothing." Never had eggs tasted so good.

Cleaning up afterward, she looked puzzled. "Turner disappear. I look everywhere." Waller knew exactly where to look: a smeared watery trail led directly to the tank of the octopus, where the shiny spatula lay in the sand.

"You have to watch Octo," Waller laughed. "He's smarter than he looks. He can figure out how to pick the lock on his tank if he sees something he wants."

Leaning away from the tank, Dolores stared at Octo's big ugly cranium, flaccid tentacles floating around it.

"Reach in and get your spatula," Waller said. "He won't hurt you."

She made a face, and there the spatula stayed.

The following Monday when Dolores came to clean, she brought a fresh-cooked meal for Waller -- *jalepenos* wrapped in tortillas, and the best black bean burritos he had ever tasted. The next week it was chicken tamales. He never knew what was next.

Late one afternoon, after she had carried the cleaning supplies, the broom, mop bucket, brushes, up the hill to the adobe tool shed, she said, "I could leeve here."

Busy repairing a pump, Waller picked up only one word. "Leave? ---" *Was she leaving?* He followed her gaze to the old caretaker's house, surrounded by tall weeds and a few shabby eucalyptus trees. Then he realized, *She means live.*

He got to his feet. "No! That old tool shed is not fit to live in."

She didn't look convinced. "I make it good again."

"No. Forget it!" Desperately, he sought a reason. "Your family would not want you living out here by yourself."

"My family, so many in a small apartment, I will ask!" Her smile was radiant.

Waller knew he had already lost.

# 6

## ~~~~~ BLUEBIRD ~~~~~

Lying by Sony's slippery body, Mara can feel his rib cage rising and falling as he breathes. He's resting, his big smooth body half in and half out of the water, enjoying the warm sunlight filtering through the dome onto the smooth cove of their rock island. Atop his back, she pokes at the bubbles that stream from his blow hole. Getting no response, she pokes at his blubbery lips. Still Sony sleeps.

She climbs to his head, slides down the smooth skin of his huge face, and stares in one open, lidless eye. Asleep or away somewhere, living in his mind images? She lies alongside him awhile, then, restless, takes the bristly brush Waller left behind and tickles the edge of Sony's beak, the sensitive place where it curves into a smile. Still he sleeps on.

She sighs, flips into the water, and turns onto her back, floating. The brilliant ball of white light above the dome moves slowly from one spoke to the next, as it does most days. She wonders if there is some giant wind-up in the sky, like the toy Waller gave her.

She sees shadows between the white ball of light and the dome, flying things, dark shapes soaring, then motionless, then moving in smooth measured rhythm, like Sony, swimming, swimming across the dome, and disappearing.

When she was small, she would swim frantically after shadows on the water, but they evaporated at her touch. Now she knows what is only the shadow of the thing, just as she and Sony make shadows on the bottom of the pool.

Suddenly she is alert. This fluttering shadow is not outside the dome; it is inside! And it is not a dark blur, but as blue as the colors in the sunlit pool, only brighter, gleaming in the sun, blue as the piece of sky she sometimes sees when the gate is open.

She watches in fascination as the winged creature throws itself against the glass dome, ricochets off, loops in frantic circles, then throws itself again against the hard edge of her world. Again and again.

She scurries onto the island, stands up, reaching up and up, though she knows the creature is far, far beyond her reach. She can hear her own voice, as always when feeling overtakes her, spilling out over the water.

Chortling encouragement and sympathy, she watches the bird struggle, until finally it flutters down and collapses in the grass a few yards away.

Eager, thrilled, Mara pulls herself onto the side of the pool, ignoring the red streaks on her arms and legs as she crawls out of the water. Her wet thrashing frightens the bird. It hops and flutters toward the far wall, where it sinks into the tall weeds, a quiet heap of blue feathers.

Mara stays where she is. She does not want it to beat against the air with its wings, does not want it to swim upward and away.

She swims to Sony, transmitting the pictures in her mind, images of the blue creature hiding in the grass. Sony, sun groggy, rolls lazily in the water, grabs her gently in his giant teeth and tosses her into the depths, as if her thoughts are too inconsequential for any other response, then he swims to see if his food trays have anything good left in them.

Back at the edge of the pool, Mara watches the quiet feathery form, and wonders -- would it move again? Or was it like the small white moths that throw themselves at the overhead lights until they fall, lifeless and dry as paper, into the water and float there, no color, no energy. Empty shells.

She wonders -- does the flying creature understand that she will not hurt it? Will it grasp the messages she is sending with her mind? Will it wait until the doors open again, and fly back to --- to where? What place does it come from, the blue bird? What is beyond the dome? Another, bigger dome, maybe, where creatures like this swim in air instead of water?

She watches and wonders until the sun no longer falls directly through the copper spokes but slants against the far wall.

As the dome darkens, she stays at the edge of the pool, half out of the water, looking at the far wall. She sees the grass move as the blue feathers fluff themselves, hears a small sleepy chirp. She feels in herself her own peaceful chirp as she falls asleep, head on her arms.

~ ~ ~ ~

When Waller went to feed them that morning, Sony devoured buckets of fish, as usual, and barked for more, but Mara, usually just as eager, showed no interest. She hung over the far edge of the pool, looking across the grass at nothing, it seemed, chattering in her clacking, garbling way. Even her favorite, shrimp and apples mashed to pulp, could not entice her. Turning to him, she increased her urgent chatter.

Waller saw nothing in the path of her gaze. "Okay, okay," he said, and went to investigate.

"Okeh. Okeh."

Midstride, he stopped. Was she imitating him, repeating his words? Feeling a leap of hope, "Okay," he said again, but her attention was across the grass.

As he approached the far wall, sidestepping overturned feed buckets and tangled hoses, a bluebird fluttered from the weeds, wings flapping. It must have flown in from the patio when he left the double doors open.

He tried to shoo the frightened bird back out, but Mara put up a fuss, shrieking and clacking, crawling from the pool.

From the lab, he brought out a dish of dry sunflower seeds, set it down near the bird, then backed off, holding his finger to his lips in the "quiet" sign Mara understood, though she didn't always obey. He hoped she would see his tending the bird as a friendly gesture, and begin to trust him.

It did seem to him that she gave him a long, appraising look from those deepset, lashless eyes as the bluebird pecked up its food eagerly and settled back in the grass.

"Okay?" He tried the word again, with no response. He had just finished some delicious French toast and went to fetch some from the kitchen. She sniffed the air, her dainty nose following the smell of cinnamon and butter. Forgetting the bird, across the pool she came. Snatching a morsel from his fingers, she thoroughly mauled it, smelled it, dipped it in her water bowl, and ate it.

"Yum," he said. "Good."

"Yum," she said, in her watery way. "Good."

He repeated the words, and she repeated her imitation. He was thrilled. This was the first time he could be sure a word had meaning for her. To reward her, he gave her another small piece of sweet French toast with a little butter.

Then she did a surprising thing. She reached out her long wet fingers and touched, merely touched, his slippered foot. The first time she had ever voluntarily touched him. He felt an unaccustomed tightness in his throat.

Before closing the gates behind him, he stood and watched for a moment. Mara lay at the pool's edge, making childlike, encouraging calls. "Bit, bit, bit." He straightened his aching back, and with a lighter step, went inside, laughing. They had one love in common. Food.

~ ~ ~ ~

*Mara is nearly four now,* Waller wrote, *still small for her age, less than three feet tall, if she could be measured without having to wrestle her down. She hates being weighed, so I don't do it often, but she is very solid, about forty pounds. Except for having no hair except a bit of fuzz on her head, she is beautiful. Her hips seem a bit more rounded lately, perhaps affected by the hormones I sometimes have to give her.*

*She has strength well beyond the ordinary four-year-old, not surprising since every movement she makes is against the resistance of water, every muscle strengthened by keeping up with Sony. She is no longer content to lag behind him; she struggles to be his equal, but she doesn't have Sony's natural advantages. He always beats her to the ball, while she squeals in frustration.*

Waller doubted she was ever going to walk anyway, so he finally decided to help her do what she did best: swim. After consulting old medical books and marine biology manuals, he designed swim fins for her, long ones for her feet, and shorter ones for her hands. Glove-like, she could put them on or take them off easily. He was pleased with his finished work, fins between her already long toes and fingers, folding and unfolding neatly as needed.

He was astonished at the speed with which she could now travel, still not Sony's forty miles per hour, but maybe twenty. She had better maneuvering ability than Sony, so as her skills increased with practice, she gave him a real challenge in their hide-and-seek and keep-away games.

He wrote in the log: *The fins also make her stronger, forcing her to thrust harder against the water. She can scissor kick so quickly now as to be only a blur of motion below the knee. I wouldn't dare try to net her; she can kick like a kangaroo. ~ ~*

# 7

## ~~~~ BA BA BURRT ~~~~

As the sun descends the wall, Mara waits, thrilled, holding her place easily with gentle fluid strokes of her long webbed feet. The miniature ritual begins: first light from the dome strikes the shadowed ledge and the dark chink in the wall, then there's a faint stirring, and finally, the lovely blue creature emerges from its cluttered nest, muttering and fussing as it fluffs, then smooths, the warm dry feathers on its rusty grey breast. It lifts its head to preen its wings, pulling, straightening each feather with its beak, a faint but expanding aura of blue and pink surrounding the perky blue head, the grayish throat and plump chest. It perches briefly on the ledge, fluffing itself, bird-murmuring contentedly as it strokes its feathers back into place.

And then --- Mara can barely keep silent --- the bird lifts its bill, its tiny chest swells, and one perfect note fills the damp morning air, a high trill followed by three short sharp cheeps. Mara counts them, one for each of her longest fingers.

She tries to imitate the sounds, but her throat feels slippery with bubbles. The bird repeats, as if teaching her, then gives itself a final shake, dips from its ledge, catches itself by its wings, and pushes through the air. Landing on top of the doors, it folds itself into a slice of blue no bigger than her hand, and disappears once more. It will come back, Mara knows. It always does.

~ ~ ~ ~

Waller carried the heavy logbook out to the decorative concrete table near the pool where he could record any new observations. The child and the dolphin ignored him. Sony raced in circles around the pool at top speed, with the girl clinging to his neckband, chortling joyous clicking sounds. Then she let go and followed Sony, diving straight down into the depths at the deep end of the pool. Minutes passed as Waller studied his watch.

When Sony emerged, shooting straight out of the water, the girl was balanced delicately on his raised beak. They tumbled, sending an enormous wave of pool water across Waller's logbook. He was sure they did it on purpose.

Quickly, he toweled off the inky pages. As the record of the entire experiment, every human-to-amphibian adaptation successfully or unsuccessfully pursued, the log was the most valuable piece of work he had ever done. When he released it, it would revolutionize biology. He had proved people could adapt to a life in the ocean. The free life of the dolphins. He would give that possibility to the world.

Now Mara crouched on the slippery wet cove, excited by Sony's antics. Ssss oh nee, she mouthed.

Waller looked up from the logbook. Was that a word? Could she actually be referring to Sony? Naming things was the first step in learning to talk. Having heard Sony's name every time he called him, had she finally made the connection?

Time for another lesson! Bringing out a bowl of freshly caught shrimp, he pointed at himself, "Waller." She reached for the bowl, but he shook his head, repeating "Waller."

She wriggled uncomfortably, swimming a frustrated circle before finally pursing her lips and blowing out a wet, "Whar." Close enough! He tossed her a shrimp. "Whar," she said again, devouring it. Pleased, he tossed her another. Then, pointing at her, he said, "Mara."

"Whar," she said, reaching for a treat but not getting one. Puzzled, she tilted her bare shining head. "Whar?"

He should not have confused the matter, should have started with what she knew. Pointing at the dolphin, chasing minnows, he said, "Sony."

When she repeated her Mandarin imitation, Sss oh nee, he pointed at himself. "Waller."

"Whar," she said, gobbling her reward. *Here we go*, he thought, *that third step*. Could she make the association? He pointed at her. "Mara."

Her eyes lit up as the idea hit her. "Rah" she said. "Mar rah." Without waiting for a treat she raced around Sony, chortling "Mahrah, Sssohnee, Whar."

One proud man, he wrote: *Besides being one smart girl - bilingual at age four, she is a world champion diver and swimmer.*

If he could give the Foundation the truth, just as it stood now, it would be the greatest breakthrough of the century. But what else would his disclosure bring with it? Notoriety? Court appearances? It was not the time. She was not ready.

~ ~ ~ ~

As Mara floats, half dreaming, she hears something... a tiny cheep from the shadowed nest. Then a fluffy yellow ball tumbles from the chink in the wall, rights itself, and flaps tipsy circles in the grass. "Peep. Cheep. Cheep. Peep."

Hearing fear and desperation in the frail sound, she raises her head and cries for help. Sony races across the pool, spins circles around her, churning the water until it flies in waves over her head, turning her calls to splutters.

She scolds him. He pretends to slink away. Circling under the water, he grasps her foot and tugs her under. She emerges quickly, her eyes seeking the yellow infant, for she knows it is an infant, recognizes somewhere within herself the call of the young for its mother.

The gates open, and Waller hurries in, barefoot, pulling a thick white wrapping around his big body, his colors showing blue and green. Fear. She clings to the edge of the pool, burbling excitement, pointing at the yellow fluff.

Waller's colors change to mauve, his big face softens as he sees the chick. Softly, slowly, he approaches the frantic fluffball, murmuring sleepily. He stoops, waits until the tiny creature calms itself, then lifts it in one big hand, holds it against his chest, and brings it to Mara.

Its tiny eyes, black, no bigger than seeds, show both fear and courage. She reaches to touch, and her wet fins drench the creature, its yellow fluff dissolving, revealing a skinny gray body. It must not like water as she does not like dry.

Waller gently closes his big hands around it and moves away from her, making sounds she now understands, like *no* and *okay* and a new one, *care full*. "Bird," he says. "Burrt," she says. "Baby bird," he says. "Baba burrt," she says.

He carries the chick back to the crevice in the wall, stands back with empty hands. She watches, silent, as the nest in the wall grows still.

He puts his hand up flat, a signal to leave it alone. Yawning, he steps carefully with his bare feet across the cluttered grass, closing the gate behind him.

Mara watches the space above the doors for the returning bluebird. She drifts off to half sleep, watching.

~ ~ ~ ~

Sony is taunting her for play, rushing at her, mocking a fierce attack. Delighted, she darts under him, races off in the other direction, eluding him. He soars, spins, comes back down with a deliberate flat fall, sending water splashing far over the edge of the pool.

She darts around the island. When he pursues she reverses direction, laughing taunts from the opposite side. He slaps the water in challenge. She dives, thrusts her feet against the bottom of the pool, driving herself straight up, spins as she surfaces, and dives again, headfirst.

He's waiting below. Enormous jaws grasp, hold and toss. She surfaces below the suspended hoop, grabs a floating red ball and sends it upward. As it drops toward the hoop, Sony leaps, pushes his snout against the net before the ball can fall through. Eyes shining, he steals the ball, carries it under water, and lies on the bottom, daring her to come and get it.

It is only then Mara sees the puddle their splashing has created beside the pool. Only then she sees a muddy bedraggled form. Baba Burrt.

Shrieking in distress, she streaks across the pool, and lifts the limp baba burrt in her dripping hands. No warm aura, no brave and frightened eyes, no beating heart. A ghastly gray thing, it is no longer a fluffy yellow being.

Waller comes at her call, stoops, takes the tiny creature in one big hand, and lays the other hand on her shoulder. She does not flinch. Taking the baba burrt with him, he leaves. She knows this is not like her deflated ball or her music box. She knows he cannot fix it.

She lies on her island, silent, the rest of the day, ignoring Sony's attempts to rouse her. She does not eat when Waller brings her food. She sleeps, dreaming that her own hands, warm and dry, curve around a soft warm yellow baba burrt, lifting him from the muddy water.

~ ~ ~ ~

The next day, Waller comes through the gates with a box in his hands. Mara sees holes punched in the lid. His step light, his colors unusually vibrant, he approaches the pool, kneels, and lifts the top of the box so she can see inside.

Mara gasps. Inside huddles a fluffy yellow Baba Burrt. Waller has made it live again.

She squeals with delight, but keeps her wet hands down and away.

Waller lifts the fluffy being from the box. It has webs between its yellow toes, just like her fins!

Holding the creature gently on his palm, he places it on the surface of the water. Mara shrieks. "No. No. No." It will drown. But when Waller removes his hand, the little yellow fluffball bobs atop the waves like a rubber toy.

"Duck," Waller says. Mara dives below the surface, sees tiny webbed feet wildly working the water. She surfaces, delighted. "Duck" Waller repeats firmly.

"Duck," she repeats, clearly and firmly. "Duck." "Duck," she says again, floating along beside it as it paddles serenely. "Duck. Duck, duck, duck, duck," she warbles, racing to Sony and back. "Duck duck duck duck duck."

Sony moves toward it, his big head tilted to focus with one eye. He opens his huge jaws.

"No, Sony. No!" Waller commands. Sony's eyes glitter with mischief. He swims circles around the tiny duck, which merely rides the waves.

Mara puts her hand under Duck and half floats him to her island. He emerges on the sloped rock still fluffy, puffing his little chest, peeping in triumph. Then he climbs into the shade of the iron figure, snuggles in the weeds beneath her feet, tucks his Sony-like bill under his wing, and sleeps.

She looks across the pool. "Whar," she says, watching his colors deepen with pleasure. "Whar."

~ ~ ~ ~

# 8

## ~~~~~ DOLORITA ~~~~~

Dolores was lonely. At night, the place was so quiet. She missed her sisters and brothers, her little nieces and nephews, their laughter and tears. She even missed Carlos. Since she was sixteen they had been drifting toward marriage, but he never had any money, spending it all on pot. "Life is a river," her grandmother would say, watching Carlos roll another joint. "But one must sometimes use oars."

Living alone four days a week and working for a man who never talked was difficult. She cried each night, feeling the emptiness of the adobe *casita* around her like a shroud. And then she would dream, tangled dreams about water and fish, maybe because Dr. Waller was letting her clean the fish tanks now, and his walls were covered with pictures of fish and fish skeletons.

One dream was so lifelike she could not forget it. She had taken the little horse out of the nearby pasture, and was riding him on a hillside by the sea, watching a dolphin frolic in the waves. Then, walking along the rocky shore, she came upon a sea nymph, tenderly young and delicate, beautiful as an orchid. While they stared at each other in rapt wonder, a dark shadow appeared, a man with a stone in his hand, whether threatening or protecting the small creature, she could not tell. She woke, overwhelmed with feelings of love and grief.

It was not an ordinary dream, not some fragment of leftover anxiety from the day. Too powerful and vivid for that, more real than life itself. A message from her very soul.

She lay in her narrow bed, watching the moonlight fall through brightly embroidered curtains, across colorful wall hangings of birds and flowers, across the red cement floor she had polished to a shine.

She'd never had her own room, much less her own casita. After Dr. Waller hauled a truckload of broken tools and junk away, she had painted the walls in bright colors and put gourds with feathered flowers on the window sill above the tiny stove.

Her family was proud of her for getting a job, especially one with an important scientist. Though Doctor Waller paid her little, the house was free, and when she bought his groceries, he paid for hers as well. She had already planted a garden, and soon there would be enough tomatoes and zucchini for her whole family. In their Tijuana apartment, they never had enough, enough to eat or enough room, especially after her brother's girlfriend, with nowhere else to go, came to live with them until the baby came.

The job was not hard. Dr. Waller liked whatever she cooked, and he only got upset if she hauled away what looked to her like junk or asked too many questions. He was funny about the pool though. Over and over he warned her, "Never go near those doors, hear?" As if she cared about his fishes.

She did wonder about the dolphins, though. Sometimes she heard them making strange noises. Do dolphins laugh? Do they cry? *Quiza.* She knew nothing of that. She would mind her own beeswax. She turned over and slept, hoping the dream would not come again.

That weekend, she took the bus to Tijuana and crossed the border to visit her Grandmother Garcia. Her cousin, Maria, picked her up in a big 32-year-old Cadillac. She was wearing high heels, tight jeans, and a low-cut top.

Older than Dolores, Maria wanted to take her to a new nightclub she had heard about. "Good dance music. No mariachis." Maria loved dancing and the attention of the boys. "I'm no much for galviscating aroun'," Dolores said. She was wearing a plain white Tee over jeans and flipflops, and wanted to stay with their grandmother. Her *abuela* was the wisest person she had ever known. They said she was a *bruja*, a white witch, when she was young. They said she could turn a flung stone around in midair, heal dying babies. Said she could know the minds of people miles away, send messages with owls.

"They say you could interpret the messages in dreams," Dolores said, when she found her in the kitchen of the apartment, standing by the heavy black stove, stirring rice. "I suppose I could do those things," she laughed. "Why not? We all live in one mind."

"*Abuela*, this dream I had, it was so real, like suddenly waking up in the future."

The old woman pushed a strand of black hair into the bun behind her neck and narrowed hawk-sharp eyes. "There are all kinds of dreams, Dolorita, most are scraps of leftovers from the day, nightmares acting out our fears."

"But this dream..." Dolores told her the whole thing, while the tiny woman nodded her head. "Portentous. There are those who have that gift, Dolorita. I am not surprised you are one."

Cousin Maria came in, pulling at her arm. "C'mon, Dolores. You can borrow my red dress."

Dolores resisted, but the dream would wait and her cousin would not.

At Club Tijuana, fringes of colored foil threw green, red and blue light across a small, crowded dance floor. The juke box, lights changing color as if by magic, played a sad song about Rosa's Cantina, where an El Paso cowboy was killed for the love of a wicked Mexican maiden. "Why do we always have to be the wicked ones?" Dolores asked.

Maria laughed, handing over her cigarettes and her sequined bag so she and her sailor could dance. "Projection," she said.

Dolores' eyes were still adjusting to the darkness when she recognized the man leaning against the back wall near the bar, partially hidden by a Donald Duck piñata. Her heart beat like a hummingbird.

Edging through the noisy crowd, she moved closer. He looked rather old fashioned in a fancy white cotton shirt and dark blue suit trousers. Dignified, like Jorge Manlove on *Sabor de Vida*, her favorite daytime television show. Handsome, suave, with a thin, aristocratic mustache. His black hair fell in heavy waves past his ears.

She could tell right away he did not belong in this place. He did not watch the girls like the other men, but stood looking out over the heads of the crowd as if at something beyond them. Aloof and mysterious, and somehow sorrowful.

Closer still, almost beside him, she saw that he wore fancy cowboy boots, stitched with flowers, exactly as in her dream. *Que extrano!* But the man in her dream had a rock in his hand. All he held now was a glass of tequila.

She tried to catch his eye, but he did not even notice her, though she could feel the stares of other men.

Breathing in courage, she pulled Maria's cigarettes out of her purse and asked him for a light. Her hand trembled, and she choked a bit on the smoke. "You have not been smoking long. You might want to think of quitting." He spoke Spanish with the formal *usted*, a hint of the aristocratic lisp of Spain.

His name was Francisco. She liked his old fashioned Mexican manners. Though he wore his white shirt with the cuffs turned back, like a working man, she could see it was quality. His hands showed he was not a working man; they were soft, there was no grease or dirt under his nails and he moved them gracefully. On two of his long tapered fingers he wore elegant rings, not Navy or graduation rings, like American men.

She did not know what to say to him and he did not help, going back to whatever it was he saw over the heads of the dancers. The silence was long and heavy. She asked for a Coke, paid for it herself, and followed his gaze as she sipped through a straw. If he was looking at a woman, she would leave him alone, but he focused on no one.

She felt foolish just standing there. "Dance?" she finally blurted out, lowering her eyes to show she was not really that forward.

"*Perdoname*, but I don't dance." He gave no explanation.

Envious, she watched her cousin dancing, her face against the cheek of her sailor-boy.

The stranger drank quickly, tossing the liquor down, drinking not to have a good time, she thought, but deliberately, without pleasure. He did not seem to be a man in love with his liquor. Why was he so aloof? And what about that rock he held in her dream?

"Your Spanish is not too certain," he said. "Born in the States?"

"No, *pero* I live there." Out of nervousness, she chattered on, sometimes in English, sometimes Spanish, about her San Diego family, and about her new job. "Old Professor Waller he strange. Always say, stay away from this or that." With a little pride, she added. "But he like what I cook, specially he like the flan my grandmother taught me. He funny, but at last, I mean at least, I do not have always to toad the line, five to nine, like many others."

Reaching for his bill, he smiled politely, and she could not tell how much he had understood. She could not let him walk away without knowing who he was. She asked quickly, "Where is your home?"

"I have no home." His eyes, deep set and guarded, held much sadness.

"No home." Hurt to the heart. "Where is your family?"

He put his wallet in a back pocket. "No family."

She could not imagine what it would be like to have no home, no noisy quarrelsome sisters and brothers, no anxious mother or grandmother, no laughing and crying nieces and nephews. "Where do you go then?" She already knew she would follow him anywhere.

He shrugged. "Perhaps San Diego. Are you driving back tonight?"

"Are you legal?"

He looked down, half smiling, as if they shared a common understanding. "Aaaaa…"

"I ask my cousin to borrow her car," she said, wondering why she was acting so brave. "It has a big trunk and California plates."

"*Muchas gracias*," he said, with a formal half-bow. "I will wait for you in la plaza in the morning. *Ocho en punto?*

Feeling very small in Maria's old Cadillac, Dolores picked up Francisco. With California plates and her cousin's California driver's license, crossing the border should be routine, but just in case, she had bought two bottles of *creme de cacao* so she could look like all the others who crossed the border to get their liquor cheap. "Don't put him in the trunk," Maria said. "They almost always look there."

Abuelita had come out to look over the stranger. While Francisco made a crawl space for himself behind the back seat, she gave him a long appraisal with those eyes that saw everything. "Dolorita, careful you not fall in love until you know you are loved in return."

As always on a Saturday night, the lines of returning traffic were blocks long at the border inspection station. At last a young uniformed inspector put his head in the window. "Bringing anything back?" he asked, his eyes quickly sweeping over her. He checked the back seat, checked the empty trunk, checked the license plates, and hesitated.

She gave him her brightest smile and handed him the paper sack with the two bottles. He winked, took one, gave the other back, and waved her on.

In a mile or two, she pulled behind a gas station to let Francisco out of his cramped space. Border crossings might be routine to her but obviously not to him. He was sweating as he climbed from the car and surveyed the streets furtively. She asked him what a gentleman like him had done to keep him from simply getting a visa, but he didn't answer.

"Where to?" she asked.

"Anywhere. Does your Dr. Waller need a hired hand?"

"You don' look like a peon. I know what hard work does. Your hands, they are gentleman hands."

"I can fix anything." He said no more. Even after he got in the front seat, he said no more.

"Okay," she said. "I'm not wanting to put my nose in your beeswax."

On the long drive to Chula Vista and the hills surrounding San Diego, he was silent, so she did the talking. She told him that she had wanted to bring some of her family to work for Waller. "El Doctor, he lower his head like an old bull an' give me such a look to scare me. If others come, even to visit, he say I have to leave. But he really need a handyman. Such a strange one."

There were always strange ones. Her uncle Tio, who would never let anyone touch his hair. Her brother Martino, who liked to go to the movies, seeing the same ones over and over, even though he knew how they were going to end. Maybe this man sitting silently in her borrowed car was another strange one.

It was already getting dark when they finally arrived. She left Francisco in the car, out of sight around a wooded bend, while she went to persuade Dr. Waller of how much he needed a hired hand.

"No!" Waller said. He was working in front of the lab, and didn't look up from the wire contraption he was fixing, a hoop-like thing. He said no when Dolores told him Francisco could fix the leaking pipes. No about the front wall, where the adobe had washed out. He said no when she said he could fix the bad wiring, but he didn't sound so sure.

Impatient, Francisco came to see what was happening. Waller exploded. "Get him out of here, right now! Do you hear me? Out!"

Francisco shrugged, put his hands in his pockets, and started back to the parked car.

Dolores stood silently, fighting back tears. She did not want to give up her job, but Francisco was fast disappearing. Placing herself squarely in front of Waller, she put her hands on her hips. "If he does no stay, then I no stay also. We are ... a... married!"

Francisco turned and sent her a shocked and angry stare.

Handing Waller the bag with the bottle of *creme de cacao*, she waved her hand at the old tanker truck, hood up, a wrench on the fender, as if she were introducing a magic act. "Francisco!"

Francisco ducked under the hood, tinkered a few minutes, then asked Waller to get behind the wheel. The big engine roared to life.

Waller got out of the truck with a scowl, half threat, half impressed.

"He fix anything," Dolores said quickly. "He work jus' for roof an' a board. No gov'ment papers to fill. Simple."

Waller gave her a shrewd look. "He's an illegal then."

Dolores shrugged. The unspoken understanding around the border was illegal aliens would work for almost nothing. On the slight chance of an investigation, the employer could simply say the worker lied.

Waller shook his head.

"Okay," Dolores said, "but never you find someone to make flan like me."

Waller opened the bag and pulled out a *creme de cacao*. He glared at Francisco. "All right. But if I catch him anywhere near the pool, I call the feds." He turned and strode inside.

Triumphant, Dolores took Francisco's elbow. "There! You have a job."

He pulled away, eyes filled with fury. "Because I am a Mexican he treats me like an ignorant savage. A girl has to speak for me."

But he stayed. That more than anything made Dolores think he was truly desperate, for never had she seen a man with greater pride.

# 9

## ~~~~~ YEARNINGS ~~~~~

Sweeping decomposed leaves from the gutters of the laboratory, Francisco saw that the roof would need much tar. Winter rains had been allowed to pool for many years, creating deep rot. Still he sang. He sang like the birds, rejoicing in the opening of the spring day. He sang because he could glimpse the sun-dancing sea through a cleavage of hills. He sang for the sound of it, his yearning soaring free as a gull, though he knew it would return to settle again, deep in his *corazon cadena*, his caged heart. He sang to ease the longing of his exile, *Preguntan de Donde Soy.* They ask from where I come. Song of the wanderer.

As a mere child he helped his grandfather tar roofs on their estate, *Los Pajaros*, near Mexico City. He remembered heating the black stuff to thick bubbles, releasing primitive fumes. Now he was only the trabajador, the hired man, and this no gracious estate, one of dignity, one of pride, but a dilapidated ruin. And who was this secretive, eccentric old man, more hermit than scientist, who treated him, Francisco Devilla, like a peon because he didn't speak English.

English! In his precocious childhood, Francisco refused to learn it. "The language of the barbarians," his beloved grandfather said after his own father lost land to Texas. Francisco learned the language of France, where his family had vacationed each year. He had enjoyed flaunting his French around ignorant American tourists.

He'd learned a little English from tourists and visitors, then from the border Chicanos who laughed at his correct, formal Spanish. They called him El Aristocrat, thought it a pose, an affectation. Except Dolores. She treated him like royalty. Dolores, little Bordita, border beauty who spoke two languages, both like a peasant.

At Los Pajaros, where as a child he dreamed of the day he would be patron, it had been necessary to learn why a roof leaked or a wall cracked. The southern climate, sun and sea, reclaimed quickly everything that was not stone, and a patron had a responsibility to his estate and to his working people.

Francisco's soul would never cease to burn with the injustice. He, Francisco Devilla, was hunted down like a criminal because he fought to hold the family estate, land that had been theirs for generations. His great grandfather had fought to keep it from the revolutionaries, but who can fight the bureaucracy? Bah. A joke of a government that came from the people but bled them worse than the aristocracy ever had, and gave them in return no pride, no art, no beauty, no religion, no culture.

Raking leaves into piles, dropping them off the edge of the roof, Francisco watched old Doctor Waller, mumbling and cursing, working on the tanker truck stalled again in the driveway below. The ancient tanker was the one job he couldn't put off, since he needed it to bring food and seawater to the marine animals he was so secretive about.

Old? Maybe El Doctor was not so old. Perhaps in his sixties, but the way he carried his shoulders, bent inward as if to protect himself, his big head down, the secretive way he lived, alone with his precious fish, all that made him seem very old. To be alone always was not healthy, as could be seen with old Waller, his pale, puffy skin, and all that flesh, soft and white as raised dough.

That and the disrepair of this place, the heaps of discarded equipment, dust encrusted, the piles of medical books growing moldy, disintegrating in the shed. No, he thought, surveying the washed-out adobe wall below, the decaying wooden gates, the patio choked with bougainvillea and weeds, it is not good to live alone. In Mexico, only misfits lived alone.

He, Francisco, could never live alone, but Bianca was his only love, and he would find a way to get back to her someday. Bianca, tall and slender, with hands that moved with the grace and pride of a flamingo. Bianca, who looked like a Paris model. "Perhaps someday I will find you in Los Angeles, the City of Angels," she had whispered as he fled on that last dark night. But how could she find him now? And why, when he had nothing to offer? Bianca would live in poverty for no man.

Below, he saw Dolores squeezing the water out of a mop. Her red nylon blouse shone in the sun. When she went back inside, her high heeled sandals clicked across the cement floor. High heels and red satin, though she had spent the morning scrubbing the professor's bathroom. Francisco shook his head. She dressed that way for him, he supposed, since Dr. Waller clearly thought no more of either of them than of the vacuum cleaner she pushed over the raveling carpets.

Poor Dolores. So young. So good. Her life was lonely, yet she said she preferred it to anywhere on earth, now that Francisco had come. That kind of talk embarrassed him almost as much as the skimpy red blouse. No matter how she tried to please him, no matter how she tried to shape herself for him, no matter which movie magazine she styled her hair from, she could never be Bianca. One was born with the blood or not.

Still, he sang. *Norte Americanos cantaban nunca.* They never sang. They listened to music on their radios, sometimes even trampled each other to hear some *hombre loco*, if he were famous enough, but they never sang as his people sang, just for the joy of it, or for the sorrow.

For days he had worked here, and never once heard music, not even the ubiquitous radio, the Tex-Mex or rockn'roll that filled and spilled over every street and alley in San Diego. Here in this California, this land of plenty, where avocados, their flesh smooth as a woman's lips, dangled from trees, and oranges hung warm and round in the morning sun, they never sang.

He stopped singing and stood still, listening to a voice, a high chant giving way to a kind of watery singing, almost as if imitating him. Could dolphins do that? Mimic like that?

He had heard other strange sounds coming from the enclosed pool, ultramodern high-frequency rapid clicking, like something electronic. Then a ghostlike creaking, like an old wooden ship.

He listened, enthralled, then sang again, louder, in a higher pitch. *Preguntan de donde soy.* A faint echo seemed to come from the glass dome. Then nothing. He hovered as close to the dome as he could get, wanting to hear again that high echoing voice.

The only doors to the pool opened from inside the patio, and El Professor kept the patio locked. The dolphin experiment, he said, was not to be disturbed. Francisco was puzzled and intensely curious. How could he disturb a dolphin? He wished only to see it. Was there only one? He was sure he heard two, but El professor would not allow questions, too arrogant to explain to a hired hand.

Dolphins had always interested Francisco. As a child, he had caught glimpses of them in the Gulf, and read many books about them. Dolores said El Professor was learning its language. Language too interested him. Language it was that brought things together or kept them apart, no one knew that better than he, an illegal alien who spoke Spanish and French, but little English.

Waller, in the driveway below, still struggled to start the engine of the ancient tanker truck. Francisco climbed down the ladder, took the wrench, and a few minutes later, with no thanks from the old boy, watched the truck wind down the steep dirt road toward the ocean.

When the truck was out of sight, he climbed back up the ladder and reached across the glass-embedded ledge with the long-handled broom, trying to wipe a space clear enough to see through, but many years of rain and mist had left the glass opaque as a worn sea shell.

He tossed the last of the leaves onto a tarp below and climbed down the ladder. As he passed in front of the decorative altar set into the front wall, he paused to brush dirt and spider webs off the blessed Mary, waiting to be restored to its niche.

On the porch of Dolores's casita, kicking the dirt off his boots, he felt his mouth turn down. The small enclosure was crowded with cheap Mexican pots in garish colors and cliche statues of little boys sleeping under sombreros. He knocked on the door, newly painted red and turquoise.

Dolores opened it, wiping her hands on a towel, her black hair blending with the cool shadows behind her. Giving Francisco her wide, white smile, she said in Spanish, "Dr. Waller will think it strange my husband knocks."

"He would think it even more strange if he knew I slept in the shed," he replied, entering the casa's one room.

Dolores lowered her lashes, rather elaborately discreet, he thought, and set plates of tortillas and beans on the table. He knew she would welcome him to her narrow bed, happy to act out the fiction that they were man and wife, but he did not want to mislead her. She had been more than good to him; he would not exploit her.

"You have never seen that dolphin, have you?" he asked, pulling a wooden chair away from the table, moving aside the vase of gaudy colored feathers that masqueraded as flowers. "Even a glimpse?"

"I tole you, he always keep that gate lock."

"But aren't you curious? Haven't you ever tried to sneak in? Never seen anything when he goes in or out?"

"I have no see inside." She sounded annoyed, perhaps because he had asked her before. She scooped cheese onto his tortilla. "Why should I? I have monkey business enough of my own."

Francisco smiled at her scrambled metaphor. "Oh? What monkey business is that?"

She lifted her chin defensively. "My job, this house, the garden, and ... meals for my husband." She gave him a short proprietary glance, trying it on, he thought, to see what he would say.

She turned on the T.V., angling her chair so that she could see her favorite Latino soap opera while they ate, and he pretended interest in the trivial drama.

There was much temptation. He was stirred by her earthy womanliness, but she was probably younger than she said. It would be good to have a woman in his life, also a great advantage to marry a U.S. citizen. He was grateful to her for getting him out of the Tijuana bars when he had nothing to do but drown in alcohol his resentment over Bianca and all he had lost. But no. He would not take advantage of her.

~ ~ ~ ~

Waller saw little of his hired hand, who quietly went about his work, but Dolores seemed less lonely since he came. Waller was glad she was happy, she with her cheerful, accepting ways, her fine cooking, and her funny malapropisms. Still he was uneasy. First Delores and then Francisco. He had to trust that the hired man, like Dolores, would have no interest in his "fishes."

How did she talk him into letting that man in? It was not just because she would leave if he didn't, although that was part of it. Or the *Creme de Cocoa*. It was all this work that had to be done, and he was getting older every day.

The morning was damp and cold. He felt the weather deep in his bones; his back and knees ached as he carried the heavy pails of fish for Sony, already barking with joyous impatience, flapping his flukes, slapping his flippers on the water. Waller flung a handful of small mullet over the pool. One soared too high, caught in the rickety basketball net.

"No!" Waller shouted as the big animal hurtled itself after the dangling fish, threatening to topple the hoop and hurt himself.

"Here, Sony." He diverted Sony's attention with a bucketful of live minnows. They darted around the pool, the dolphin happily in pursuit.

Mara was watching eagerly from her island cove. He decided to postpone her feeding until after her lessons. She worked harder for treats if she was hungry.

~ ~ ~ ~

"Sssohnee." Mara taunts Sony in a jeering tone, chattering and clacking. Because he is drowsy, she is one point ahead of him in the game with the ball. She chortles as she takes a sharp piece of rock and scrapes another line into the concrete. She has one more mark now than he.

Sony comes up from behind, thrusts his huge head under her arm, pushes her away. Scornfully he spins, deliberately tossing the ball well outside the pool. It barely misses Duck, sleeping in the shade of the avocado tree, head under his wing. Duck squawks in protest, opening wide his yellow bill. He waddles awkwardly out of the way, his long neck and shimmering blue-green head pulling him like a toy. He settles near the wall, quack-grumbling, and smooths the bands of iridescent blue on his brown wings until they shine like chevrons. Mara marvels still at his plump soft beauty, marvels that the tiny ball of web-footed feathers gradually, day by day, disappeared into a scrawny brown thing, which then became this handsome, glittering Duck.

Duck quacks loudly, a demanding succession of falling calls, starting on his loudest note, ending with a cranky croak, then waddles, mallard head gleaming, grey chest puffed, back to his favorite shady nook under the trees. Waller calls him Crankee Duck.

Mara dotes on Duck. Each time he lifts his plump body on those feathered arms and miraculously flings himself upward, flapping over her head, she is amazed.

When the bird shadows come in groups and she hears their distant honking, she watches him. He flies overhead, circling under the dome until they are gone, then he reluctantly eases downward, returning to the ground quacking querulously, as if he has not found what he is looking for.

Mara fears what he is looking for is a place where he, like Bluebird, can fold himself up and slip into Outside.

~ ~ ~ ~

# 10

## ~~~~~ TANGLED PATHS ~~~~~

Dolores sang as she went about her gardening. Francisco not only worked hard for Dr. Waller, but he still found time to make her life better too. He fixed the pipes under her sink and emptied out the drip can, along with a drowned mouse. He fixed the place where the leaking roof sent water stains down the walls. He fixed up her bike, and got out the rusty old one stored in the woodshed years ago. She hoped they could maybe ride together someday.

Pulling weeds from the newly emerging carrots, she moved on to the squash. Soon, with his help, she could have a larger garden, and if she got permission to bring the goat her uncle had offered, they could maybe rent the pasture next to the road. The lonely little horse would have company.

Missing her nieces and nephews, she dreamed of having a child someday. -- No. No child. Francisco had cleaned out the old woodshed to make a place for himself, and there he slept, over her protests. But that could change.

"Your garden is doing well." Francisco had come up behind her. She felt the blood rush to her face, as if he could read her thoughts. "Si," she said quickly. "These real tomatoes, not like the ones in the market, all white inside."

When they went in the house, barely big enough for a bed, table, and couch, it felt so intimate, the two of them in its small warm space, that she went shy and speechless. Ducking into the tiny bathroom, she changed out of her dirty jeans.

Checking under the kitchen sink, Francisco emptied the drip can, along with another drowned mouse. He examined the stains on the kitchen wall, where the roof used to leak. He would find time to get it painted soon.

Dolores came out of the bathroom wearing her shiny red blouse and tight jeans, her hair swept up to show dangling red earrings. After turning the small black and white TV from the news to a soap opera, she started supper, heating tortillas and a spicy topping on the two-burner stove, chatting in her usual Spanglish about her family, endless cousins and nieces and nephews. He wasn't paying much attention until she said, "We could have a kid..." His mouth went so dry he couldn't swallow.

"What!"

"A baby goat, silly. You think I mean a child?" She laughed, giving him a sly look from under lowered lashes. "But if Mother Mary so willed, I would like a child someday."

"Someday," he stammered. "Someday when you marry..." He knew it wasn't the answer she wanted. In the awkward silence, his eye fell on the book he had given her. Seizing the opportunity to change direction, he said, "Tried Lorca yet?"

"Lorca?" She was grating cheese. "I'll get some at the market if you want."

"Lorca," he repeated, trying perhaps too hard to be gentle. "He is a famous poet, like Shakespeare, only Spanish." He gave her a nudge. "Shakespeare. Romeo and Juliet, you know?"

"I know who is Shakespeare," she snapped.

"Pardon me." He watched the television in silence while she cooked.

When they sat down for dinner at the wobbly table, she said, "I have been thinking."

He nodded politely, wondering if she ever really thought, or merely imitated whatever affectation she learned from TV, or from her friends, whose constant topic of conversation seemed to be what boy had called or hadn't called, who really liked whom, what girl had married or had a baby.

Tugging bits of paper from her napkin, she gave him a long reproachful glance, like the one he'd seen on the screen a moment before. "Sometimes I don't think you like me, you know?" Her voice broke. He was afraid she was going to cry. "Boys – men -- have never, you know, ignore me as you do."

He didn't know what to say. Once, coming in after knocking, he found her stretched out on the couch in a sheer nightgown. Ignoring her had not been easy.

Twisting the napkin, she lowered her eyes. "My friends, they ask. I tell them it is the way of the aristocrat. He does not have passion like us. He is more --- how you say ---cool."

Ah. Bianca would never agree with that. "Dolorita Mia," he said, leaning toward her. "My little sad one." She pushed him away, but he held her arm and made her look at him. "I would not impose on your generosity. You should not offer so much when I can offer you so little."

"I have offer you nothing." She threw the napkin aside and stood up, head high, backing away, knocking the vase of colored feathers to the floor. Now he had injured her pride.

They sat at the wobbly kitchen table and ate their tacos in silence. Finally she looked up from her plate, her dark eyes questioning. "Francisco, in the night I dream of a slender woman with a teasing smile, a woman -- how can I say -- elegant looking, her hands, she moved them -- how can I say -- like birds."

Francisco was startled at how closely her dream resembled the way he thought of Bianca. "So you are psychic?" He laughed uneasily.

"Maybe. Maybe my dreams mean nothing, but sometimes I think I am like my grandmother. She dream other people's dreams and then they happen."

"Well, my best and worst dreams happened when I was awake." He laughed again, somewhat bitterly, and eased down on the couch, almost sitting on a book. "What's this? *Encyclopedia of Dolphins*. In Spanish!"

"I see it in San Diego. I buy it for you," she said, proud of her find.

"*Gracias, mi amiga.*" Genuinely pleased, he began reading while she stayed nearby, planting tiny seedlings in pots on the broad window casings.

"Listen to this, Dolorita. Millions of years ago dolphins were land animals. Though they returned to the sea for some unknown reason, they have retained many characteristics of homo sapiens."

"Sapiens? Monkeys?"

Was she smiling?

"Homo sapiens, humans."

"Oh." Crimping soil around a tiny plant, she murmured, "There. You will grow to a beautiful chrysandymum."

Francisco continued reading aloud. "Like man, dolphins depend on lungs to breathe, and can stay under water only a few minutes at a time, though more than humans. They have a larger brain than man, 1,700 grams to man's 1,450 grams. Ay! Think how intelligent they must be!"

Dolores nodded and reached for another plant.

"And kind," he continued. "If one is sick, the others will lift it to the top of the water so it can breathe. Did you know dolphins are even more conscious than people? For them, breathing is a choice, they can start or stop any time they choose. For us it's just automatic. Even dying is by choice for a dolphin. For no apparent reason, one will just leave the group, dive to the bottom and die. Imagine. Completely by choice."

"It is not only dolphins can choose," Dolores said. "Say you will have a heart attack at forty, and you will have a heart attack at forty. My Grandmother, she know."

"Ay! It says here, for males erection is a choice, not something that just happens. Ha. I'd like that!" Immediately he knew it was a stupid thing to say. Avoiding her sudden look of interest, he quickly went on reading. "Their skeletal structure is similar, having a pelvis, femur and tibia like ours..."

"Tibia. Leg bones," she said with some pride.

"Yes. And their flippers even have wrist bones and five finger bones, just like our hands. It says here they can stand on their flukes, their tails, using them like feet."

She laughed. "Can you jus' see them standing aroun' the bottom of the ocean like a bunch of business mens at the water cooler."

"Fascinating," Francisco said, closing the book.

"Yes," Dolores said sadly. "I hear Dr. Waller's lonesome one cry sometimes, just like a child."

Recalling what he had heard earlier, he sat up straight. "Scientists keep records," he said. "Have you seen where Waller keeps his records, perhaps a journal or a log book?"

"I see him writing sometimes in a thick book with a green cloth cover, watery, very old I think."

"Water marked," he said, alert. "What's in the book? Laboratory notes, figures? What?"

"*No se.* He never live it around."

"Where does he keep it?"

"I tole you, I don't know! You are always after me about that. It is all you care about."

"You must have seen something in all this time. Aren't you even curious?"

Smarting under his criticism, she turned back to her plants, refusing to answer.

Sorry, he stood and said goodnight. "Thank you for the book. It was very good of you to think of me."

Crossing the garden and the irrigation ditch, he saw the shine of patent leather by the sandy path. Curious, he stooped and pulled out a high-heeled shoe, the insole eaten away with age, *Hecho in Mexico* imprinted on the sole. Just one of Dolores's old shoes. He tossed it away.

Dolores watched from the kitchen window as Francisco moved through the eucalyptus, watched him climb the hill behind her house until he stood on the bluff overlooking the ocean, where he stayed for a long time, looking south, she imagined, toward Mexico. Homesickness, she thought. How hard it would be, so far from everything he had ever known and loved. Remembering the beautiful woman in her dream, she feared in her heart that he would one day not come back from his lonely wanderings.

She sighed and turned away from the window. What of the stone, the stone in his hand? A dream. It meant nothing. But a woman? She had worn her sexiest blouse tonight and made up her face so nice, and still he looked right past her.

She cleaned up the few dishes and put them away. Keeping up the fiction of marriage was almost enough to make her happy, for now. Never had she thought to meet a man like Francisco, a man with such grace and elegance. Maybe he would never love her but what mattered was that she loved him, had given her heart to him the first moment she had seen him in the dark shadows of Club Tijuana. Cousin Maria called it "Martyrdom."

Dolores did not agree. Some day her love would warm him as the sun warms the sea. *Quando Calliente del Sol.* When one loves enough, can the other long resist?

~ ~ ~ ~

Waller examined with satisfaction the repair job Francisco had done on the crumbling courtyard wall. It had been good to have Dolores here; she took care of him and showed no curiosity about the animals. But then she had brought Francisco.

He felt easier knowing the man was no longer on the roof, even though he couldn't possibly see through the dome, covered with years of sediment. The ledge on which it rested was embedded with broken glass. Maybe he was paranoid to think an illiterate Mexican laborer had any interest in what went on in the pool.

The man was well on his way to taming the tangle that threatened to take over the place. He seemed a good man, drank a beer now and then, loved his woman, did his work. That was his life, a simple one and a good one, judging by the way he always sang. Al envied him. His own life had become more and more complicated since the night the dying woman dragged herself up the road, bringing her unborn child. How long ago? Five years? If anyone found her now---

As he entered the patio, he saw the Mexican in the courtyard carrying a shovel toward the heavy doors that opened to the pool.

"Hey, you!" He caught the smaller man by the shoulder and whirled him around, throwing him back against the wall. "What'nhell do you think you're doing in here?"

The man tried to explain in Spanish, pointing to some broken tiles, but Waller wanted no explanations. Stabbing an index finger into the other man's chest, he bellowed, "I told you never to go near those doors."

Again he jabbed Francisco's ribbed undershirt. "You no go there!" he yelled in exaggerated pidgin English. Then he pointed at himself. "I, me, only, savvy?"

Francisco's smooth features showed nothing.

*That is the way of these Mexicans. Tell them and tell them.* No *comprende*. Waller shoved him through the outer doors and threw the bolt.

In the *sala*, rummaging behind the wooden bench, he found a blue nylon athletic jacket, eaten by mice, and a yellow slicker, so stiff it cracked. His old target pistol was still in the pocket. He took it out and made sure it was loaded.

Perhaps what was in that pool had to be disclosed, but if it was, by God, it was going to be he himself who did it. In his own time.

# 11

## ~~~~~ DILEMMAS ~~~~~

It was a beautiful day. Dolores and Francisco took their bicycles out of the shed, hers a red Schwinn, his a rusty old wreck, and looked down the dirt road that wound to the ocean. He complained that they would have to push their bikes more than a mile to get back up the steep hill.

She laughed. "You don' wan' to push, what you want is one of these." Nodding toward the pasture where the dappled gray horse lazily cropped grass, she took an apple from her backpack.

"Not mine I hope," Francisco joked, as the horse lifted its great head and mouthed the apple out of her palm, juices dripping.

"I ride him once. All the way to the beach. Bareback." She stroked the long smooth muzzle and gave him the other apple. "My grandmother she talk to horses. I see her do it. Talk even a wild one right up to her hand." She patted the horse goodbye, they got on their bicycles, and headed down the back road through the woods, skidding on ruts, braking on every turn. When they rounded the last curve, the road straightened out, and they coasted all the way to the beach.

While Dolores spread a bright colored serape on the sand and laid out mustard, ketchup and hot dogs, Francisco, preoccupied, hardly noticed what he ate, tugging at weeds tangled in his bicycle chain. "Have you seen anything yet?" he asked.

She gave him an impatient look but did not answer.

"What kind of food he takes to the pool?"

She hugged her sweater around her shoulders against the cool wind coming off the Pacific, and shook her head.

He pursued it. "You must see something, you clean the tanks, bring him his dinner."

Dolores shrugged. "I tole you, nothing special. Buckets of live fish, sardines I think, sometimes lettuce, fruit sometimes."

"Fruit? We must look in the book and see if dolphins eat fruit." He tossed the mangled weeds onto a bed of yellow dandelions and rotated the pedals. The bicycle made whirring grasshopper sounds as the chain turned.

He tapped his fingers impatiently against the bicycle frame. "Your El Doctor almost shook my teeth out when he caught me working in the patio this afternoon." He clenched his jaw. "Who does he think he is, to treat any man so?"

"But he tole you never to go inside." Dolores picked dandelions and wove them into a crown.

"How am I to be the *trabajero,* the caretaker, if I do not go inside!" He sat silent a long time. "Something very wrong goes on in there. . . perhaps something evil."

"Evil? No. It is only he is a strange one, a scientist, uptight, as they say. Many Norte Americans they are uptight. My grandmother say they like to make things exactly their way. They cannot, but they try. She say that is just how they are."

Francisco nodded. "*Verdad* . They leave no room for life." Still El Doctor's reaction seemed extreme to him, even for a *Norte Americano.*

Finally, head down, Dolores said very quietly, "I see where he keep the book ... how you say, the records?"

Francisco stood up. "Where, Dolores? Tell me!"

"In the lab, in the bottom desk drawer."

"Dolores! Bueno, bueno, bueno!" He gave her a rewarding hug.

She wasn't as happy. "Always he keep the drawer locked."

Francisco took the crown of flowers and set it on her head. "Dolores, I am going to learn what El Doctor guards so jealously."

"No, Francisco! We will both lose our jobs, or worse!"

But he was already mounting his bike. "I am the man. Trust me."

~ ~ ~ ~

The winds off the coast carried in a morning squall. Waller couldn't take the tanker down for fresh water, the road would be too muddy, so he took a rare free moment to sit at the desk with his monthly science magazine. Reading, he scoffed with contempt. *Long stretches of DNA in the human genome and that of animals are either the same or similar. Research on sequencing the genome of people and animals is blurring the line between them.* So neuroscience and genetics was finally admitting there is no black and white divide between people and other animals. About time. Well, his work would hasten that along, if he could ever release it.

He leaned back in his desk chair, the rusty spring giving its familiar groan, and reached for the university/government forms. Grants meant progress reports, and until he was ready to disclose what he really had here, he could only report what he learned from the dolphin, without the disclosing the girl. He had hundreds of tapes of dolphin language, stacks of corresponding notes, but to compile it, there was never time, and anyway he didn't like what they had done with the information they already got from him, training dolphins to carry torpedoes, for instance. Trusting creatures, they were sent with explosives right to a target, and blown up along with it.

Smoothing out the forms, he stared at a blank page. He sometimes thought they would fund the toenail cutting habits of toads, as long as he filled out the forms properly, but he could think of nothing to add to what he had already told them, could think of nothing but what he could not tell them -- the truth of what he had achieved, this marvel living in the pool with Sony.

He must somehow satisfy the Foundation. He was already late getting them in, and he didn't like thinking of what he would be forced to do if he didn't get the grant extended. Without funding, he simply could not keep up with the deteriorating equipment or the mounting needs of the growing animals. The dolphin alone weighed three hundred pounds and consumed twenty pounds of fish each day. His own money was almost gone.

From outside, he heard the whine of the pump that fed fresh water to the pool. Not good. The report would have to wait. A nagging inner voice responded, one that always seemed to have a distinctly female tone. "Come now, Al, you're only justifying your procrastination." His mother's voice, though she had died years ago.

After he installed the new pump, he stopped to check the hoses by the shed, all of them brittle, patches on patches. He heard Dolores call her husband, and watched the Mexican back down the ladder, envying the broad shoulders that flowed into narrow hips. Sliding his hands around his own girth, hearing laughter from the couple's little house, he felt twinges of jealousy, old familiar feelings of being left out. Long ago he had learned to convert them to something more satisfying -- being the one who excluded others. He tapped the pistol under his lab coat.

First Delores and then Francisco. How much longer could he keep his secrets? More and more he was feeling a sense of impending doom; something, sometime, had to give.

Pump working, he went to clean up the pool, hosing off the walks, picking up the junk that accumulated in the grass. The avocado tree needed pruning, and the rambling bougainvillea had crept up the walls, driving its shoots through widening cracks. The copper mermaid hovering over the island was mostly green now, only her curved hips still had a slight copper shine. Her beautifully scaled tail was hidden in weeds.

Although the pool water was still a bit murky, he could see Mara and Sony lying on the bottom. Sometimes he thought they competed for who could stay under longest. She had developed a large set of lungs. He set his stopwatch. Her record was eight minutes, already surpassing humans.

As he worked, his eye was arrested by two rows of nearly identical scratch marks, the size of matchsticks, on the edge of the pool. He knelt, studied them closely. Nothing he had dragged across here could have left such marks. Then he noticed the piece of stone lying next to them, and compared it to the marks. Yes, Mara had made them. She was keeping score. Mara was counting!

He had tried teaching her to count and given up. Abstract numbers had no meaning for her; it only mattered who had the most marks, Sony or her. Symbols. A thrill of pride, a sense of hope welled up. If she understood symbols, maybe he could teach her to write.

Suddenly Mara was at the edge of the pool, crying out, "Duck! Duck! Duck!" Waller hurried to the wooden doors and shut them, scolding himself for his carelessness, but Duck was already out, already lifting on flapping wings, heading over the patio walls.

Mara's cries turned into wails as she crawled from the pool, teetered uncertainly on arched feet, and stumbled after him. But Duck was gone.

Waller cringed as she slid back into the water, murmuring, "Duck," in a very small voice.

Sony went for the blue and red ball and nudged her with it. She would not play. He nudged her again. When she only murmured, "Duck," he slipped under her just as he did when she was very small, ferried her carefully to the island and laid her on the grass under the outstretched arms of the mermaid.

Waller turned to go back and fill out the forms, the joy of her achievements already fading.

~ ~ ~ ~

Mara watches the heavy doors open each day, but Duck does not come back, no matter how she hopes. Where is Duck? She knows he is not a lifeless shell, like the moth or the baba burrt. He is not gone in that way. He is Outside. What is *Outside*? she wonders.

And where is Bluebird? Is there another, larger dome, outside this one? Do Duck and Bluebird fly across it every day, like the sun? Or like the round white light that moves across the dome at night?

Waller is inside. As he carefully closes the doors behind him, she sees only a glimpse of another wall, and above that, a wide blue arc. She knows that is Outside.

She has an unsettling thought. Could she, like Duck, wait her chance, wait for Waller to come through the doors, and rush past him? But then what? She could not fly over the wall into that piece of blue. Even if she could, would she just disappear as they did, Bluebird and Duck?

Trembling, she remembers what happens when she crawls too far from the pool, the terrible frightening feeling of being out of the water, unsupported. She feels almost faint, remembering. And she knows from lying on her island too long on sunny days, what happens if her skin gets dry. The sun shrinks the skin of her skull. The sun will shrink her into a dead husk, like the moth floating on the pool.

Shuddering, she drops deep under the soothing water, where sun filters in streaks from the wavy surface, and searches for Sony.

He is resting on the bottom, feeding his dreams with images of endless water, pale green algae waving in tree-like stalks, swarms of colorful fish, swimming way, way, above him, like birds in the sky.

~ ~ ~ ~

The next day was still damp and foggy, and Waller felt that way too. He was sorting the good hoses from the bad when he was suddenly drenched by a huge wave from the pool. Gasping, he turned to see what Sony was doing. The dolphin rushed full speed across the pool, then shot straight up from the water and dropped with an intentional flat splat next to the girl, washing her off the island. She laughed with delight, laughter that seemed to him, almost flirtatious. He felt his back stiffen.

Stunned, he stood and watched them play. Smaller than her years, about sixty pounds, she already had the curved hips and small breasts of a pre-pubescent girl. Years of living in a kind of green house, directly under the sun, might have forced early physical maturity. The hormones he used probably added to the problem, as did the oil in her food. And a problem it was! There was no mistaking the tone of Sony Sonar's excitement.

The dolphin took another fast run, and when he seemed about to ram Mara head-on, he turned at the last moment so that his soft white belly brushed hers. The girl, minnow quick, swam away, laughing as the dolphin caught up, and again ran his belly against hers, making high excited clicking sounds while simultaneously blowing soft wet bubbles from his blow hole.

Waller watched with growing anxiety. With dolphins it is the female who initiates play, signaling that she is in heat by starting the amorous games. Clearly, Sony was courting her, and without knowing it, Mara was encouraging him. The dolphin had been sexually mature for years now, and something had triggered his awareness that she had reached that passage also, though she was only six.

Waller calmed his fatherly sense of outrage, but a sense of emergency remained that had nothing to do with ethics or morality. Mara was emotionally and physically still a child, and could be seriously damaged by the amorous intentions of a powerfully driven, three hundred pound dolphin.

He pulled a whistle from his pocket and blew a long sharp set of high-frequency signals. At first, Sony was too excited to respond, but after another sharp blast, he came to Waller and lay his bill on the edge of the pool, his eyes shining like a happy puppy. Waller scooped a live fish from a tank, and tossed it in the pool, hoping to distract Sony, cool him down, while the girl floated at a distance. When Sony chased the fish in a cat-and-mouse game, Waller was reassured; if Sony was so easily distracted, there was no immediate danger. But danger there was.

As he had written in one of his published articles, dolphins often spend as long as three days in courting; playing, nipping, caressing, even wrapping their flukes around one another, whirling on their tails like dancers. There might be a warning, thirty minutes or so of frantic whistling, crying and dancing. Then suddenly, in an instant, the male will charge the female, wrapping his huge flukes around the lower part of her body, penetrating her with his spade-like dorsal fin. Thirty seconds later, it is all over.

Sony would have to go. There was no time to make arrangements to sell him, though he was worth thousands, nor did Waller want to attract attention by putting him on the market. He would have to release the dolphin to the sea. Domesticated as he was, he might hang around the cove below, giving Waller time to make better arrangements. If not, Sony would eventually adapt to the sea. Other dolphins would help him; they responded to distress signals from miles away. Sony would have to go. Now.

# 12

## ~~~~~ GLIMPSES ~~~~~

The next day was bright and clear. A sharp breeze carried the scent of honeysuckle. The ocean mist had lifted earlier than usual, and the sun warmed Francisco's shoulders. Birds quarreled joyfully in the lemon tree. He whistled as he worked, imitating their songs.

He was pouring tar on the lab roof when El Doctor climbed into the tanker cab, as he did every Thursday, going after water. This time, Francisco could hardly contain his impatience. The starter cranked and cranked. The old man got out and lay across the fender with a wrench, ignoring Francisco's offers to help. Finally, he eased himself out from under the hood and looked up at Francisco with an uncomfortable, lopsided smile. "It's no use."

Wishing the rusty old hood would swallow the man like a great jaw, Francisco climbed down the ladder, reached for a wrench, and after a couple of cuts with his pocket knife, replaced the fuel line. He gestured to Waller to start the engine. It ground twice then caught with a roar. Waller backed out the driveway without even a grateful nod.

He was usually back in an hour. In minutes, Francisco was over the courtyard wall and working at the lock of the big double doors to the pool. Dolores came out of the lab and fluttered around him anxiously. "What if he forget something and come back?"

"He never comes back before an hour." He slid a plastic card against the spring-loaded bolt, but the heavy iron lock would not give.

"But what if this time he does?" Shaking her head, she went back inside.

Francisco tried his pocketknife, then an old skeleton key he'd picked up in the shed, and finally a heavy wire. Nothing worked.

He went into the laboratory, looking for clues. What exactly was in the pool that had to be kept so secret? He had never been inside. A wave of stale air, smelling of fish and mold, engulfed him. The green light of fish tanks gave the room an eerie underwater glow. Amid a ballet of kelp, an octopus floated, its tentacles waving aimlessly.

"Ugly beast," Francisco grimaced. Its head was as big as his, and its hooded beak looked like a man's testicles. "Who would want to spend their whole life with such things?"

"The octopus, he has three hearts," Dolores informed him with some pride. "El Doctor say he has a brain better than most inverteb...?"

"Invertebrates. Without spines," Francisco laughed, giving her a teasing shove. "Three hearts and spineless, like some women."

"So you think," she said, pushing him back.

He fastened a sponge to a stick and prodded the beast, which retreated to the far corner of the tank amid a cloud of blue-black ink. Though the animal could back no further, Francisco poked again. In a flurry of water and ink, the creature snapped off the end of the stick. "Clean as an axe!" Francisco stared in shock, and prepared for another parry.

"Francisco. Go!" Dolores stared at the overhead clock.

In another tank, a bright, silver-blue fish darted past what seemed to be a jagged rock, but suddenly the rock opened, snapped shut, and the fish was gone. Francisco shook his head in disbelief.

"That rock is no rock," Dolores said. "Like my grandmother say, nothing ever what it seem." Fussing, pulling at his sleeve, she shadowed him as he prowled about, kicking at overturned buckets, cardboard boxes, plastic feeding trays, moldering scientific journals.

Opening a warped door to a storage room, he found an empty glass tank, some three feet tall, with water rings near the top. "What do you suppose he kept in that?" Too big for fish, too small for a dolphin. A chill went through him. He tugged at a brittle tube, so old it fell off in his hand.

"Now you've done it," Dolores scolded, wide-eyed. "Now he know someone here."

Ignoring her warnings, he opened the door to El Doctor's bedroom. "*Repugnante.*" The heavy drapes covering one small window were so old they were disintegrating. The bed was a bare gray mattress, sheets and covers kicked into a wad at the foot. A pair of gray pajama tops, worn thin across the back, hung from the metal bedframe. Dirty lab coats and undershirts, reeking of fish, were piled in a heap in one corner.

Every remaining inch of space was filled with boxes of books and magazines, many of which, he realized as he poked through them, were not scientific journals but medical journals. One fell open at a yellowed article Waller himself had written, something about Dolphins and evolution. He put it back. Behind the dresser, he discovered a framed medical school diploma, and another with a later date, granting a Ph.D. in Marine Biology.

He turned to Dolores, standing in the doorway, fretting. "Why is your Professor, with his two degrees and high honors, living like this?" He kicked the pile of dirty laundry.

"He is catching you in here, is what he is doing. Then I will be out of a job, and also you." Dolores stomped back to the kitchen, making it plain she would have nothing more to do with his illicit snooping.

As he was closing the bedroom door, a crumpled piece of paper caught his attention, an invitation for Waller to speak at some kind of seminar: *Proofs of the One Mind: an opportunity to experience psi data.* He tossed it back on the floor. Obviously Waller had no respect for psi, whatever that was.

Dolores looked out the window. "I warning you! He catch you, we both in hot soup."

"Relax. I'll hear that old engine long before he gets even close. Trust me."

*Que fregado.* What a mess. Finally he spotted the old roll-top desk and tugged on the bottom drawer. "You say he keeps the logbook here?"

"Locked," Dolores said, pulling him away. "You go now."

He opened the top drawers and groped through their contents. Nothing of interest. Precious time was passing. "Go!" Dolores said, pushing him out the door.

Outside, he grabbed the ladder and climbed up to the roof. Across the top of the glass-embedded wall supporting the dome, he had laid a heavy plank, a bridge. On hands and knees, he crawled across and studied the dome's gritty surface. Sure enough, a hairline crack ran across one curved pane of glass, nearly invisible under the grime. With his pocketknife, he dug along the copper edges. It was risky. If the curved pane should break - - what would happen then, he did not know.

From below, he heard a strange cacophony of creaking, clicking, and barking. Then a hollow thumping. He supposed that would be the dolphin, pounding a flipper flat against something. But then, laughter --- he was sure it was laughter! --- followed by a high lilting scale, like a girl's singing.

Feverishly, he worked to pry loose a small glass triangle, thick and heavy, only a few inches long. At last, he pulled it up, carefully set it beside him on the wall, and peered in the opening, his heart silent with anticipation. Even the birds seemed to quiet down, the breeze to stall.

Through the branches of an avocado tree, he looked down on a cluttered, untended enclosure. In the center was a huge, kidney-shaped pool with a small island on one end. He caught his breath. A figure -- mermaid? -- was poised on the island as if she were about to dive! No. It was only a life-sized brass statue, though beautifully realistic, rising up from its weedy base.

Surrounding the pool, what had once been a gracious formal garden was now an overgrown weed bed, strewn with broken hoses, discarded cardboard containers and rusty equipment. Stainless steel tanks, overturned buckets and feeding pails lay in the weeds. More were stacked by a shed that probably housed pumps. A bright red beach ball bobbed on the water, and wind chimes tinkled with the waves. Dolphin toys, he thought.

The pool was littered with leaves from overgrown shrubs and trees. He could see nothing at all under the surface. Where was the dolphin? He whistled as one would for a dog, but nothing surfaced. Taking a quarter from his pocket, he dropped it in the pool, and as it splashed, a silver-gray shape some six feet long made a lazy glide just below the surface of the water. A curved dorsal fin cut a clean swath across the length of the pool and disappeared again.

He searched his pockets for something that might encourage the dolphin to surface again, but found nothing that wouldn't rouse El Doctor's suspicions. Taking a chance, he took a cleaning rag from his belt loop, tossed it down, and a moment later, a smiling bill snatched it and whipped in circles around the pool, flying the rag like a white flag, flukes cutting above the water like the tail fins of an ultra modern plane.

Francisco whistled and clapped. The big animal spotted him, lifted his bulk partially out of the water, poised, as if expecting food. When none came, he dropped back under the surface, where Francisco could make out the gleam of his white belly turning in the depths.

Excited, he crawled back across the plank and down the ladder. "It's just a dolphin, like he said," he told Dolores.

Dolores crossed her arms. "Satisfied? What you expect?"

"But I also heard something like laughter, feminine laughter."

"Big imagination. It is maybe a baby dolphin you hear, *verdad?*"

From a tray in the stainless steel refrigerator, he took a frozen fish, small enough to drop through the hole but large enough to attract a dolphin.

Dolores scolded. "How do you know it can eat fish so cold? You are going to make us big trouble. Here, give me." A fan whirred and clanged noisily over the big commercial oven while she warmed the fish.

Francisco paced. "If there is only a dolphin, I don't understand what all the secrecy is about."

"I tole you, he is just that kind of man," Dolores said, handing him the fish, still cold but thawed.

With the noise of the fan, they had not heard the truck, already turning in the driveway. Dolores stared at Francisco with wide eyes, took the fish and shoved it back in the refrigerator.

Francisco grabbed a mop and thrust it into her hands. "Stand in front of the door --- tell him the floor is wet. Keep him busy." She gave him a frightened I-told-you-so-look as she fumbled with the mop.

Francisco was carrying a tar bucket toward the ladder when Waller got out of the truck and came around the corner. "I thought you said that job was finished."

"Si, pero...." Francisco shrugged, suddenly unable to think of any words.

Waller looked in the bucket, banged the stick on hardened tar. "You're not going to patch anything with that."

Francisco struck his forehead, as if realizing how stupid he was, and started back around the house. Waller shook his big head and walked away.

When he had gone inside, Francisco scurried up the ladder and crawled across the plank. Anxious to put the glass back where it was before Waller discovered the opening, he moved too hurriedly. His knee hit the unstable piece, knocking it through the hole. It splintered on the tiles below.

Perhaps in response, a dolphin's shimmering form leaped from the water, spinning in the sun, sending water flying. Francisco stared. On the back of the dolphin, riding the dolphin, effortlessly, as if completely at one with it, was --- what? A mermaid?

Then it was gone, leaving only turbulent water, choppy waves. It was just an instant's vision, but he <u>saw</u> it, a marvelous human-like figure. Blue-white, almost translucent, violet in places. Impossible as it seemed, it was a girl, or something very much like one!

Below, the wooden pool doors rattled. Francisco pulled a branch over the opening, and crawled off the ledge, praying Waller would not look up.

He could not believe what he had seen, a girlish figure, gently curving hips? It must have been some trick of imagination. A mermaid? Did it have a tail? No, he could not say he saw a tail, just long legs, webbed feet grasping the dolphin as it sailed high into the air, slid back into water and disappeared, taking the rider with it.

He went about his work, cleaning, storing tools and buckets, but his mind was feverish. The image leaped from the water again and again, hairless, blue-white, fluid female lines, beautiful in the clean cool way of department store mannequins before their clothes and wigs are fashioned.

Hairless as a fish, skin a silvery blue-white. Perhaps it was a woman in a white swimsuit and a tight swim cap? No. Nobody could, hands free, ride a dolphin straight up out of the water like that, disappearing again under water, not even a trained Sea-World stunt rider.

As a child, he had read stories of mermaids, sea nymphs, dangerous creatures whose songs lured men to their ruin on the reefs. Of course he had known such stories were mere entertainment, but he had loved them as he loved the myths he studied in school, myths of gods and goddesses who rose from the sea. The memory of what he had seen merged with what it might have been. Dolphin and woman blended, and in his mind, the image of mermaid---*ninfa marina*---persisted.

Again and again, his eye went to the dome. He yearned to throw the plank across the ledge and verify that he had not hallucinated, but it might be days before he would have another chance to go up on the roof. If Waller spotted the broken glass, and saw the place where the glass was missing, it might be never.

In his excitement, Francisco wanted to tell Dolores what he had seen, but he wasn't sure what her tender heart might make her do --- break into the pool on a rescue mission? Tell the authorities? Warn Waller of what he was up to? No, he couldn't tell Dolores.

Gullible creature that she was, believing in astrology, in spirits, in dreams, whatever, she might immediately go telling all San Diego there was a mermaid in the pool. Then, if El Doctor was doing illegal or immoral experiments, no telling what the man might do to protect his secrets.

# 13

## ~~~~~ EDEN LOST ~~~~~

Francisco's secret separated him further from Dolores. He knew by the way she followed him with her eyes when she thought he wasn't looking that his preoccupation was not lost on her.

He hung about the domed pool on every pretext, but he quit talking about it, quit asking questions, quit speculating aloud about the mysterious sounds that sometimes soared in high frequency spirals, then fell into quiet, almost human murmurings. In response, Dolores seemed to withdraw as well.

He missed the light chatter about her niece learning to walk or her grandmother's archaic wisdom, the same chatter that used to annoy him. But right now, he had more important things to think about. He needed to find a way to get into the pool area without getting caught. One little chink in the glass was not enough. He needed to see clearly what he only thought he saw. He needed to know the truth behind the vision.

He was reinforcing a roof drainpipe so it would hold his weight without pulling loose next time, when Dolores came hurrying around the back of the lab. "You have to come! El Doctor, I think he is after the dolphin --- I see him push the big stork rig..." Stork rig. The crane Francisco had seen rusting outside the lab!

Just then a shriek pierced the air, raising the hair on Francisco's neck. He raced around the building. Chaos was breaking loose under the dome. He could hear El Doctor swearing and cursing, the high shrieks of the dolphin, and watery screams that sounded almost like a terrified woman, drowning.

The patio doors were propped open, and El Doctor, soaked through, chest heaving, blocked his way, brandishing a huge wrench. Just as Francisco tensed, ready to disarm him, he handed it over. "I was looking for you. Wait here." Francisco took an eager step toward the pool, but Waller had closed the gate behind him and a bolt slid against the other side.

Another heartbreaking cry, then silence. The tumultuous thrashing of water and dolphin was over. Why? What happened?

After excruciating minutes, the doors opened and Waller came out, pushing a wheeled crane ahead of him, an ancient contraption like the ones used on the docks in Mexico to load heavy cargo. A wooden pallet hung suspended, and on that, wrapped in foam rubber, fastened with straps, a dolphin lay like dead.

Waller put his hands against his lower back and groaned. "Don't just stand there. Help me get this damned thing to the tanker."

Francisco put his weight behind the stalled rig and got it moving. As Waller reached behind him to swing shut the gates, Francisco stole that moment to slip a stick under them, a stick just big enough to keep the lock from clicking into place. After getting the rig outside, Waller locked the patio gate behind them, but Francisco had been over that before.

"Careful now, dammit!" the old man warned as the crane teetered. "If this thing tips we've lost him." So the dolphin wasn't dead, maybe tranquilized.

While Waller steadied the crane, Francisco pushed it across the potholed parking area until it rested against the tanker, the pallet balanced over the open portal. Waller used his weight for balance while Francisco cranked the heavy pallet up over the truck, then Waller climbed up, tipped the pallet, and the dolphin slid out of the rubber casing, landing with a splash in the tanker. The whole process had taken about an hour. In all that time the pool remained deathly quiet.

Francisco climbed up, closed the hatch, lowered the pallet, and moved the crane away from the tanker, knowing the aging man could never have handled the load without him.

"There, he'll be all right now." With obvious relief, Waller leaned against the truck, a glimmer of actual appreciation on that heavy, dour face before he got into the truck, patting his hip as if he might be carrying a weapon. "You stay away from the pool."

"Si, Señor." Francisco hung his head, demonstrating the proper respect. When the truck was out of sight, he took a run at the front wall, boosted himself on the Madonna niche, threw himself across ground glass, and dropped onto the patio.

His wedge had worked. The lock had not caught. Pulling open the wooden doors, he went inside. The dolphin must have put up a terrific struggle. The entire area was soaked. Water ran down the walls several feet from the pool. All was silent. Soft light fell through the milky dome and glanced off the quiet surface of the pool, where a bright colored ball bobbed lazily.

Where was she? He knelt, peering into the cloudy water, but saw nothing. He walked around the pool, surveyed the island, but found no sign of whatever had been the dolphin's playmate, the one who laughed like a child, but only minutes ago, shrieked like some demented creature.

She had to be here. He checked the shed, looked under an old tarp that covered some buckets. Nothing. Completely bewildered, he turned to leave. It was then he saw a limp, lifeless blue-white form, sprawled face down behind an open gate. She must have tried to follow the dolphin.

He knelt next to her, afraid to touch her, afraid to frighten her, afraid that even a gentle touch might hurt this fragile creature. She lay very still. Was she dead? He closed his fingers against her wrist, and felt a pulse beating under a layer of plump soft flesh.

Her limp fingers separated, fan like, disclosing folded webs between them. Her feet too were webbed. Examining more closely, he realized that both feet and hands had fins pulled on like gloves or socks, matching her skin and fitting so well, they were a seamless part of her.

Her skin was not like his, but damp, not slippery, but exquisitely soft, with a filmy covering, somewhat like a fish, extremely thin, almost translucent. Her long, narrow feet were like curved extensions of her ankles, and the skin on the bottom of her feet was as smooth as that on her face, so evidently she did not walk. She must live entirely in the water.

What was she? Not quiet human, yet certainly no mermaid. Very small, fifty or sixty pounds, he guessed, a pre-adolescent female but hairless as a baby. She wore no clothes, and her nudity had a child's innocence. Lifting one of the long narrow hands he saw the palm was scraped bloody, and her forearms as well. Probably from pounding on the wooden doors.

A sea creature? What if she could not live out of the water? He scooped her up, surprised to find she was heavier than she looked. Suddenly her white-lashed eyes flew open, and before he realized what was happening, she threw herself out of his arms and scrambled for the pool, each move tearing at her knees. He grabbed her, and in one motion, tossed her high over the deep end of the pool. She arched instantly into a graceful dive and went straight to the bottom.

There she lay in the depths, motionless except for flowing movements sideways, like a fish makes to hold its place in current. He watched in wonder. Minutes passed, and still she did not come up for air. He remembered what he had read of dolphins, that dying, or in grief, they simply quit breathing, sink, and drown.

Wrenching off his boots, he dove deep and grasped her around the waist with both arms. She flipped free of him, throwing him into the side of the pool with one blow of her long, muscular legs, knocking the breath out of him. He climbed out of the pool and sat gasping on the tiled edge. From the force of the blow, he knew she was not dying, but from the shadows on the other side of the bronze mermaid came the high, pure cry of grief.

Calling soft consoling words, he crept closer. She moved to the opposite side of the island. The crying went on and on. He sat listening for a long while, stunned with amazement. *She has no hair, she knows the water like a fish. She has webbed feet and hands, but there are no mermaids,* he repeated to himself.

If she was human, then she must have been kept in watery captivity since she was very young, perhaps from birth. Had an innocent child been used for inhuman experiments? The thought filled him with outrage. No matter what the reasons, in the interest of science or for something evil and demented, there could be no excuse for what had been done to this beautiful child.

He heard a truck in the distance, laboring up the grade. Could Waller be returning so soon? He must have gone no farther than the beach. Had he set the dolphin free? If so, why?

Francisco leapt to his feet, scanning the area for any tell-tale signs that might betray his intrusion, then he grabbed his boots and left, locking the pool doors behind him.

When the tanker pulled up out front, he was doing what he hoped Waller, with all his prejudices, would think a very Mexican thing -- sitting by the courtyard wall, playing the guitar, singing *Pregunto de donde soy --- They ask from where I come ---* as if to console himself for some unimaginable loss. He was singing for her, the girl who lay in the shadow of the mermaid, inconsolably weeping. He hoped his song would comfort her.

# 14

## ~~~~~GUILTY INNOCENCE~~~~~

Dolores and Francisco had bicycled down the winding dirt road that led to the beach, stopping as always to give the gray horse carrots from the garden. Off the hill, along the coast road, they pedaled through dunes covered with plumed grass. In a tidal pond, a heron stood on one leg, head tucked under a wing. "Like my cousin Mario," she laughed. "If you don't look, whatever's coming can't hurt you."

They pushed their bikes down a narrow path to a small sandy cove hidden between the rocky cliffs. Francisco pulled off his shirt and sat down in the sun. Dolores warmed oil between her palms, kneading it into his strong back with firm healing strokes, speaking in Spanish.

"Francisco, where were you last night?"

He felt his back stiffen. "What do you mean, where was I?"

"I went to call you, but you were not there. Where were you?"

"I sometimes wake early and walk up the hill to watch the sun warm the fog away."

Her hands moved across his shoulders. "You are very tense."

"Am I?"

"Francisco, I know you are sick for your home, but is that all? Sometimes I see how you look at me like when I think Lorca is a cheese. Because I have only seventh grade, you think I am not good enough for you? Is there somewhere you go at night? Is there another woman? Is that why each time it gets warm between us, you talk about dolphins? You sleep in the bicycle shed, but sometimes I look, and you are not there. Is there somewhere else you go for love?" It came all in a breath, like something pent up. She wiped her eyes, smearing mascara in dark circles.

He turned and gently wiped away her tears. "I am homesick, yes, Dolores. I often wander at night, remembering my friends, my home, my beloved Mexico. It is not easy for me to be an outsider, a nobody. It has nothing to do with you."

"Francisco, what happened to your clothes the time you left them in the shower? They were wet and smelled of fish."

She caught him completely by surprise. He'd forgotten his wet clothes after he found the girl in the pool. "I...I'd been cleaning some fishy buckets after that rainstorm."

"Ridiculous. And why do you ask all these questions about El Professor? About the pool? Why do you act like he is evil? Francisco, is he keeping a woman in there? Is that what I hear that you say is a dolphin?"

"Now who is ridiculous?" Francisco laughed. "You read too many of those border tabloids.... Woman gives birth to fish.... Absurd." He turned to her, but she moved away from him. Francisco waited quietly, and when she continued to massage his shoulders, he changed the direction of their talk. "That Waller, I still do not like the man. There is something evil about him."

She smiled. "I have known him for years, never have I see him harm even a fish. Even an ugly octopus he likes."

"Many people are kind to fish, dogs, birds even, but are cruel to their own kind," Francisco said.

"He is always kind to me," Dolores countered, "Even you he gives a job. My grandmother tell me when we don' like another, we are only looking at some part of ourselves we don' like. We can try to kill it or love it."

"Your grandmother has lived too long," Francisco said, tired of hearing her easy philosophy.

Dolores stood up, brushing sand off her jeans. "I myself am going and ask El Doctor what he keep in that place," she said, hands on hips.

"No, Dolores. Don't."

"Why no? If it is something evil or against God, should we stay here? I have heard of white slavery, have read of evil sex experiments. I will not work here if he is evil as you say."

Francisco held her arm. "Dolores, he will have me deported if we make trouble."

"But what if it is not true? Then he will only laugh at me and tell me the truth." She turned to go.

Francisco hung onto her wrist.

She faced him, not with anger but with determination. "Then tell me what it is that you do at night. Tell me what it is that you know."

Francisco took a deep breath, raised himself to his full height, and looked down at her. "Dolorita, I am the man. A man does not tell a woman everything. I have my reasons. And tomorrow morning you will work as if nothing happened and you will say nothing to El Professor about your suspicions. I will tell you when I am ready to tell you. You must trust me, or we have nothing."

"Tell me then, Señor Mystery, why you are afraid to be sent back to Mexico? It happens all the time, you give them a false name, they let you go on the other side of the border, you find your way back in a week or two. It is a ---- what do you call? --- a mouse and rat game."

"Dolores, for me it is not that simple. Mexico is my home, home of my father and grandfathers, but I can not go back."

She spoke more gently. "If you miss your country so much, Francisco, I would go back with you. We two can find a way to live always."

Francisco was touched by this woman so different from any he had known before. So vulnerable and yet so solid. Honest yet kind. Independent yet dependent.

He touched her hair. "I know you would do that for me, little one. But I cannot go back. Ever. I did not tell you everything because I did not want to frighten you."

"Trouble over your father's land, you told me. That is nothing. Everyone has things like that, fights and things."

"Someone was killed. Someone important."

Pulling a towel around her legs against the cool wind coming off the ocean, she sat down next to him. "You can tell me, Francisco."

He gazed over the water. Rising waves signaled an offshore storm. "*Bueno*. I will tell you, my little one." He had only meant to divert her from the secret in the pool; now he heard his voice thicken as memories overtook him.

"My family estate had been struggling some years. There had been a drought, crop failure, nothing that our hard work and patience could not cure. But when grandfather died, the debts were called in and I came home from a summer in France to learn my father owed thousands in gambling debts to a crafty bureaucrat named Olivera, a weasel who preyed on the weaknesses of others, the lowest kind. My father asked Olivera for more time. Olivera refused, but offered to play him one more game --- This to a compulsive gambler! --- The winner, Olivera, of course, took all, including the family estate."

"Oh, Francisco!"

"Probably he cheated. He was known for that. Prided himself for that. Anyway my father, a gentleman unused to the ways of such low lifes, went home and shot himself with my grandfather's dueling pistol.

"Oh, Francisco!"

"A degree from Academia de Paris is less than worthless in Hermosillo. I went to work in a fancy nightclub, Club La Luna, like a nobody, waiting on those who used to be my friends. There I learned well how to charm, how to dance like light on water, and above all, how hungry for love the ladies are, under their disdainful glances. I observed Olivera's ways as well, particularly how he lusted after women of aristocratic families the way some men lust after race horses.

"One evening when his wife was visiting her family in the States, he invited me and my fiance, Bianca, to a private party at *Los Pajaros* --- _my_ *Los Pajaros* --- Imagine the nerve, inviting *me* to what had been my own family estate." Francisco spit with anger.

"He wanted to gloat. And he wanted Bianca. She was proud and would fight off poverty any way she could, just the sort that Olivera would prey upon."

Drifting into the past, Francisco almost forgot Dolores. "What a joy Bianca was, playful and challenging, witty and sensuous . . ." He caught himself when he saw Dolores' pained reaction.

Her chin went up. "Women you buy like property make you yourself their property."

Waiting a moment, head down, he went on, turning from grief to anger. "Olivera, who had more to drink than was good for him, taunted me before Bianca. He offered me what he had once offered my father; one game of cards. This time the winner would get *Los Pajaros* and with it, Bianca. But I had learned something else in that club, the ways of those who gamble without honor."

"You cheated," Dolores said in a small voice.

"I was prepared to cheat, but Olivera lost to me."

"So - you took your revenge?"

"Not revenge. Justice! Olivera, a pig worse than a muskrat, would not honor the bet. He laughed and said it was just a game. After my father had honored with his own life just such an agreement!"

"But you too cheated."

"I said I was prepared to cheat. Luck was with me, and I won honestly."

His voice deepened as he revisited the darkest hour. "That night, I waited by the gates of *Los Pajaros*, decorated with intricate peacocks of wrought iron, gates my grandfather had built himself. I waited with his pistol, the same one my father used."

Dolores' hands went to her mouth.

Francisco went on, his eyes on the distant sea. "I can still see his arrogant expression as he pushed through those gates, thinking they were his. I knew he always carried a gun, but I had him where I wanted him. He would either sign the estate over to me, as honor demanded, or try to kill me. I could then shoot him in self defense. Either way, I would win."

"Francisco... you killed him?" Dolores's dark eyes had a look in them he had never seen before. He looked away.

"Oh, Francisco." Her voice was hushed with sorrow. He could almost feel her shiver.

"I wasn't..." Francisco's voice broke. He breathed deeply, collecting himself. "I wasn't prepared for the shock of it, taking a man's life." He hardened his jaw. "By the time the police arrived, Olivera's gun was gone; his friends had seen to that. And they put on such a show of grief, making me out to be a vengeful loser, the sympathy of the people went with Olivera's family. You know what it's like; the ones with the money win."

He laughed bitterly. "If it had not been for the influence of my childhood friend, Rodrigo, a wild and crazy medico with the necessary bribes, I would be in prison yet."

"And Bianca?"

"What could I offer her now?"

"Aiee, Francisco." Dolores stood and put her hand on his shoulder. "You must let the past go. We must accept what life brings or be always in pain."

Francisco shoved her hand away. "Your simple homilies! How could you know what it's like to lose everything when you have never had anything!"

Flinching, she turned away. He was immediately sorry. "*Madre Mia*, Dolores, you make me feel so guilty."

Dolores took his hand and gazed at him, the clouded sunset reflecting off her lovely face, but when he leaned to kiss her, she shook her head, no longer in awe of him.

# PART III

## EDEN LOST

# 15

Sony is not. Mara lies at the bottom of the pool, eyes open, seeing nothing but the slow movement of the water, light filtering marble-white from a remote and uninviting surface. Her hands float beside her, as if disconnected, yet she knows she is gently tended by the water, by her own closing and opening fist of a heart, by the uninvited expansion and contraction of her lungs that will soon force her to surface.

A familiar resonance. Waller's heavy tread on the ground above sends mild shock waves through the water. She eases closer to the shadows of her island, comes up for air, drops again. A stiffness comes over her. Her whole body locks in resistance.

She feels the vibrations of the feeding tray knocked against rock. His form sways above her, the white coat, yellow through the water, the glow of his life barely discernible, even less than a leaf. Yet he had overpowered Sony, taken him Outside.

Emerge or die. She surfaces in the far shadows, waits warily until he leaves, then the knowledge closes in again, leaving her with only her own emptiness. Sony is not.

She pulls herself onto a slick, smooth rock and lies inert. Into her emptiness comes a rhythmic sound, like the strumming of fingers on taut strings. Like the red music box, the sound lifts and falls, lifts and falls. A deep voice makes words swim and sway like water.

She rests her head on her arms, and for a long time lets the strumming humming sounds synchronize the movement of her breathing. She sometimes makes music with Sony. But Sony is not.

She pulls herself out of the water near the lifeless metal being that guards her cove. She stares up at the face, metallic, yet under the softening light, familiar, arousing strange feelings, tender, yet sad. Green copper streaks run from the lifeless eyes, flow down the soft face, down hips rounded like her own, and fall in rivulets down the rock.

That face arouses in her a strange recognition, a vague longing. When she was smaller, when she was afraid, when the white coat had the net, or moved too sharply, or when the horrifying roar moved into motion beyond the front wall, she would hide behind the metal figure as if it could protect her. She would crawl up on the boulder, reaching out to arms so like her own that she sometimes thought they might reach down for her.

Even though she knows the softly curved figure is even less alive than shadows, she still imagines the arms are moving, swooping down to pick her up.

She twitches, drops deeper into shadow. Darkness is. Her whole being is darkness. Sony is not.

~ ~ ~ ~

Francisco slipped into the woods and took his favorite path up the hill overlooking the ocean. He had gotten away with his pool visits one more time. The rising sun dappled the hills in soft ocher touches, bringing the gray oaks to life. Birds quarreled in every tree. The sight of the sea, just visible over the trees, comforted him. Water, with no dividing lines, connected him with the land from which he had been exiled. He felt the familiar longing, for home, for position, for respect, for what should have been his birthright. For Bianca, the woman who might have been his. The longing, as always, came with a burning anger that sometimes erupted in ways he could not anticipate.

He must think of a way to free the girl before something terrible happened. It occurred to him for the first time that he might risk calling Rodrigo, get his advice as a doctor. Maybe with more knowledge, he could do something for her.

Dangerous. There was always a chance the story would be too good for even Rodrigo's tongue to hold on to, and someone would come looking for Olivera's killer. Still, Rodrigo would never intentionally betray him and he might have answers.

Getting his bike, he headed down the back road, braking on every turn before getting to the pay phone at the public beach. One red-suited jogger plodded along an otherwise deserted cove. He propped the bike against an abandoned hot dog stand, barely avoiding a loop of barbed wire, reminder of the days when most of this land had been cattle ranches, and before that, Mexican cattle ranches.

He dropped some coins in the pay phone, gave the operator Rodrigo's office number, and fed in most of the quarters in his pockets. Rodrigo answered the third ring. "Como?"

"Even if I am holding my severed head under one arm," Francisco said, "You are going to tell me now to take two aspirin and come to your office at nine."

"Francisco! *Dios mio, mi amigo!* My God, it's good to know you're somewhere, anywhere, and that you are all right." He was laughing with excitement, and so was Francisco, so good it was to hear the voice of a friend, to chatter in Spanish.

"Where are you?" Rodrigo asked, then interrupted himself. "No, you don't have to tell me. I don't have to know."

"So the Olivera's still have the police dogs after me, *verdad*?"

"*Pues*, as the man's image grows, so does the price on your head."

"Rodrigo, I never felt good about what happened. You know that."

"Francisco, the bastard asked for it."

He had to ask. "And Bianca?"

A long silence. "Married," Rodrigo said.

"Not to Olivera!"

"No." A half laugh. "Not that bad." Then gently, very firmly, "Me. Bianca is married to me."

Francisco winced, leaned his weight on the shelf, feeling as if he were in a canoe, drifting further and further from a beautiful island on which all his friends laughed and loved.

He tried to lighten his voice. "Well, Bianca was never a patient one."

Rodrigo agreed. "She is like water that runs over stones in a brook." Francisco could hear the love in his friend's voice. He traced with his finger the black outlines of the gaudy wiener on the hot dog sign, the dripping catsup like his heart's blood.

Rodrigo, after giving Francisco time, found his old buddy voice. "My biggest threat is the romantic memory you have become. I wish you were around to dribble a little chile on your shirt. Flawed mortal that I am, it's difficult competing with a specter."

The operator cut in. "Your three minutes are up, sir." Francisco fed in the rest of his quarters.

Beyond, a car stopped, and he saw a woman walk down to the beach with a girl in a swimsuit and a small boy who dropped into the sand, filling a red bucket, turning it over, making a sand castle.

"Go ahead, sir," the operator said.

Francisco drew a deep breath. "Rodrigo, I telephoned because I need some help."

Rodrigo was eager to compensate. "*Claro.* Anything."

"It's going to be hard for you to believe everything I am about to say, amigo, but trust me, I am quite sane and quite sober." He launched into an abbreviated account of everything he had seen and heard, from the moment he first saw what he thought was a mermaid, to the nights he spent teaching a water-child to trust him.

"My God," Rodrigo breathed. "*La Nina Aqua! Increible*! I have heard of attempts to keep fetuses alive in water but I can't recall one ever lived. Of course there are many cases of newborn babies who swim under water, but this is truly incredible. Why is this Doctor Waller keeping such a secret?"

"Rodrigo, it is a human being we are talking about, not a medical marvel. Not a laboratory experiment. Waller's insane, of course. *Loco in cabeza.* Evil. I have to get her out of there, maybe find a cove, a sheltered pool somewhere warm until she learns to live on land, but I don't know what her needs are."

Rodrigo asked questions that Francisco had no answers for. How long could she stay under water? How long out? How much did she weigh? What did she eat? What was her body temperature? The temperature of the pool? Her pulse? Blood pressure?

"Get me that information and call me back. Meantime, I'll do some research...."

Rodrigo's voice became less professional. "Someone totally adapted to the sea. Mother of God, the possibilities of that! Francisco, if I fly up there could I see her? Could I bring a colleague?"

Francisco was speechless. He had not considered such a reaction. "I could be on a plane in an hour," came Rodrigo's voice, insistent. "Where are you?"

"Your time is up, sir." The operator's voice.

Francisco hung up the receiver and leaned heavily against the building a while before getting on his bike.

One tire was going flat, probably a barbed wire puncture. While patching the tube with some glue and plastic, he caught a glimpse of the beach from beneath the hot dog sign. The boy was wading in to his waist, and heading for deeper water. His mother stood screaming at him. "Franklin D. Junior, you come right back here!"

The girl pointed to something beyond a breaking wave. "There it is, Mom. See? I told you I seen a dolphin."

A few yards off shore, Francisco saw the arched back, the dorsal fin, disappearing flukes. Could be just a common dolphin, he thought, not unusual in these waters, though not normally so close to shore.

Franklin D. treaded water a few yards out, rising and falling with the waves. The mother was screaming. The dolphin surfaced near him, and Francisco saw it was not a common dolphin, but a bottlenose, its Donald Duck bill giving the appearance of laughter.

To the mother's terror, the sleek gray form swam straight for the boy, caught him in his teeth and tossed him in the air. Pushing him in a frothy rush to within five feet of shore, he disappeared in the waves.

The boy's face was a cross between wide-eyed wonder and stark terror as his mother dragged him from the water.

Yes, this was Waller's bottle-nosed dolphin. Only a domesticated dolphin would be that friendly. Was he staying close to where he had been released because he could not adapt to freedom? Or was he trying to stay close to the girl, perhaps even communicating with her in ways we don't understand?

As Francisco pedaled back up the steep dusty road, Rodrigo's words rode heavily on his heart. Married. Bianca was married. The same birds sang in the brush, the same plumed grass waved by the inlet, the same blue sea shimmered in the distance, but it all seemed very dim and unimportant now. He felt a kinship with the dolphin, its longing heart so much like his own.

# 16

## ~~~~~ DESPERATION ~~~~~

Mara is dying without Sony, Waller had to admit it. He tempted her with all her favorite foods -- apples, shellfish, hardboiled eggs, but she would have none of it. Each day, she slipped off the island into the pool as soon as she heard him coming. If he tried to net her, she fought him, dragged herself out, and huddled against the far wall. She had finally stopped the pitiful whimpering, which tore his heart out, but her will to live, her joy and vitality, were gone. Sometimes she lay on the bottom of the pool so long he feared she would drown.

A dish of shrimp in one hand, he rapped sharply on the tiled edge of the pool, Mara's feeding signal, but she was no Pavlov's dog. Refusing food was not stimulus-response behavior. This was deep grief.

Despair flooded him as he watched the pitiful, grieving child. For years she had been happy, more happy than any suburban child in her protected home, always playful, full of life, innocent as Eve, with Sony her Adam, and he, Waller, a frightening but benevolent God. Now it was over.

He regretted what he'd had to do -- could only imagine the terror she must have felt as Sony darted around the pool, clacking frantically, trying to avoid the tranquilizer darts, the horror she must have felt when Waller clamped Sony onto the pallet and hauled him away. Gone. Forever. How was she, a wordless creature, to understand that gone didn't mean forever?

Now she lay on the island, unmoving, wary, more frightened of him than she had ever been before. Her eyes, normally lustrous, looked dull in the purple shadows of her gaunt face.

Knowing she would not eat the food he brought until he left, and maybe not then, he left it in her feeding dish, and went back inside the lab.

Hours later, he checked again. She had eaten nothing. What could he do that he had not already tried?

He heard a distant screen door slam, Francisco leaving Dolores' cottage after, no doubt, a fine supper --- and the man was singing as he went back to work on the clogged roof drains, singing in that magnificent tenor. *"Cuando caliente del sol."* Something about the sun. His own voice was like a crow, always had been.

Resentfully, Waller watched the grieving girl emerge from the depths, lift her head, and gaze toward the dome as if the man's singing was the music of angels. He, Waller, had tried everything to arouse her from her grief, and just the voice of that peasant brings her to life! "To hell with her."

Wild animals were tamed by first starving them, so that when food was finally given, the captor was seen as a savior. Hostage behavior showed the same results. Though he didn't like thinking of her as a hostage, maybe that's what he should do. He took the food away, and returned to his work inside. If she got hungry enough, she would eat.

~ ~ ~ ~

The pool had been quiet all day. Francisco could not forget the small form he'd found sprawled near the heavy doors. How light she had been in his arms, how innocent and vulnerable. With a chill, he recalled her shrieks and cries as the doctor wheeled the tranquilized dolphin from the pool, the endless keening of her grief. He could only imagine her great loneliness, her inconsolable sorrow, for now she had nothing at all to love. Not to love, Francisco knew, is to die in your soul.

When he saw the lights go off in the lab, and was sure Dolores was sleeping, he crawled across the plank and quietly, working from the small open triangle he'd cut earlier, inched a large wedge of glass away from the copper frame and began work with the cutter. Slow work, with little light from a sliver of moon, but his imagination drove him on --- a nightmarish vision of the pasty-faced professor trapping the girl, she floating in a laboratory jar like a pickled brain. Rage growing in his heart, he worked feverishly.

Dolores said all life was choice, but the dolphin girl had no choice. Confined to a few hundred feet of watery space, she was totally controlled by Waller, her life and even her death. Without language, there was no possibility of consoling her, promising rescue. Without language, Francisco pondered, there is no future, there is only the present and the past, and given her present, how could she choose to live?

By the time he'd cut out a piece of the dome large enough to get through, light was already crawling across the hills to the east, the dawn hush broken only by a few small birds fussing in a nearby oak. From the brushy canyon behind the lab, a mourning dove called its sad soft elegy.

Extremely careful not to be heard, he finally moved a large wedge of heavy glass aside, and lay it on the ledge. The pool lay below, a dark kidney shape, unfathomable, undisturbed. Like a miniature moon, a light shone yellow-white under water so calm, even the wind chimes were silent. His heart filled with dread.

Crouched on the plank, he estimated the distance he would have to drop. If he landed on the concrete, he was finished. If the avocado tree broke his fall, he could make it. But how would he get back out?

He got down off the roof and returned with the extension ladder, cringing as it rattled against the flat roof, and carefully lowered it through the hole in the glass. It was just barely long enough.

He edged down the rungs, but stopped suddenly when he spied a dark silhouette. Only the bronze mermaid. Stepping off the ladder, he approached the pool, singing softly. Nothing. Still as death.

Finally, to his relief, he heard a stirring of water behind the rock island and there she was, in the shadows, clinging to the edge of the island, prepared to flee. He inched toward her, reassuring her, crooning cadences, hoping his pale blue shirt, his jeans and bright red scarf would mark him as different from the man in the white laboratory coat. Did she have that kind of discriminating intelligence? Or was any human the enemy?

Her eyes, without lashes, were large, deep set, surrounded by shadows that made them seem even larger in that small face, in that bare, perfectly sculpted skull.

She allowed him to come closer. He took a bar of chocolate from his pocket and held it out to her, talking, murmuring, humming bits of song. She showed no interest in the food, but his voice seemed to hold her. Perhaps she had heard him singing earlier. He edged closer. Her gaze never left his face. Those eyes --- fathomless --- showed only the apathy of despair, the languor of grief. He felt a fresh wave of fury toward El Professor for taking away from this isolated child the only thing she loved.

From the lab came the sound of a flushing toilet and a door closing. What was Waller doing up? Francisco, preparing to run, set the chocolate at the edge of the pool, and the girl, frightened, slipped under the surface and was gone.

Francisco waited. Silence. El Doctor had gone back to bed.

The girl came circling back, undulating slowly just under the surface at a safe distance; then her shining white head emerged, and quick as the raccoons on his grandfather's ranch, she snatched the chocolate and swam to the island. In seconds, she was reaching for more. The place smelled of fish, but having none to give her, he pulled an orange from the nearest tree, peeled it, pulled off a segment and tossed it to her. She fingered it with long, webbed fingers, sniffed it, and dropped it in the water.

He picked a ripe avocado, peeled it, and slowly ate it, making a great show of pleasure while she watched him closely.

He peeled another and tossed some pieces onto the island. She mauled it in her long, webbed fingers, sniffed it, and finally ate it.

Francisco stood helplessly, pulsing with frustration. In very few minutes, the sun would be up. He couldn't just leave her like this, but he couldn't carry her away either. He didn't know if she could walk, or talk, or how long she could stay in, or out of the water. He didn't even know if he should have given her chocolate, or what else she could eat. He had to have the logbook.

Reluctantly, he started up the ladder. Remembering the avocado peels, the orange peels, so neatly knife-cut, a sure give-away, he went back for them. By the time he'd pulled the ladder up behind him and replaced the glass, there were lights on in the lab. He lay the ladder flat on the roof, dropped beside it, and waited until he was sure he had not been discovered.

Finally, he climbed down, elated. He'd gotten away with it.

She had responded to song, and she was eating. He could hardly wait for nightfall to come again.

~ ~ ~ ~

Waller still hoped that something good could come of this. He wrote in the log: *Once freed from her association with Sony, the girl could transfer her dependence to me, learn to trust me again, and finally, show a real interest in learning human ways. With only me to depend on, she might even learn to speak fluently. A creature that could speak both dolphinese and English; what a breakthrough that would be!* If he could get her to eat.

*Perhaps without her dolphin playmate, she will be motivated to walk, but that is less likely. The very structure of her feet has been formed early by the action of muscle on water. They function now much like the tail flukes of a dolphin, not to walk but to swim.*

*But with Sony gone, I might be able to keep her out of the water for longer periods. She might lose the panic she goes into whenever she leaves that fluid, supportive environment.*

Waller put the pen down. Maybe there was still hope for her to live on both water and land, but before he could do anything, she had to eat! She had to *want* to live.

He had only begun to look at the unfinished grant forms, late again, when he heard the honking of the mail carrier on the main road. "All right, all right," he muttered, slowly ambling out, not even glancing at the face of the driver as he signed the receipt. Another registered letter from the Foundation. Standing in the road, he read it, expecting complaints, still, the contents stunned him.

*Due to lack of evidence of sufficient progress ... the Foundation has determined that funding will be discontinued as of this date. It is with regret, since early reports and your previous reputation gave us high expectations . . .*

*We will reclaim inventoried laboratory equipment and animals within thirty days ...*

Waller leaned heavily against the gate. He thought he had pieced together enough haphazard notes, translations and computations to placate the bureaucracy. Yes, the last report was late, but he had been certain they would give him one more extension. They always had.

Thirty days. He felt as if he had been told he had only a month to live -- it took some time to take it in. He stood staring at the mail truck as it disappeared down the road, taking away his last hope for continuing his sheltered, isolated life as it had been for years.

He fairly staggered into the kitchen and downed a scotch. Thirty days to vacate the laboratory, get her out of there before some official came and saw what he was really doing with their dolphin money -- before they saw who or what was in the pool. There was no way out.

He collapsed on the bench by the pool. He could not possibly keep her without financial support. She must have seawater, continually changed. Special formulas, extremely expensive.

And now, since she wouldn't eat, she would need intravenous feedings. Even more difficult, since she would never allow it. She would have to be tranquilized.

He sighed wearily. Through overgrown trees, patches of light fell through the dome, sparkling on the quiet pool.

What if he let them have her? What if he placed an anonymous phone call to the Foundation, *come and get her*, then disappeared. At first there would be a burst of attention when they found what they would surely call a dolphin girl, but in time they would try to turn her into a normal ordinary girl.

He tried to picture Mara taking her place among normal six year olds, laughing, playful, freckle-faced girls, hair streaming down their backs, biking in the sun, chattering gaily. It was impossible to see among them this small blue-white hairless creature, whose skin dried and cracked after mere minutes in the sun, and whose whole body, muscle, tendon and bone, had developed for the thrust and kick of swimming.

After people got tired of the work, the expense, the frustration, she would be shoved into some institution until a little carelessness solved the problem for them and she died of pneumonia, infection, or loneliness.

And what about him? Who was he without his work? Like the girl, he had been maintained for years in a kind of experimental tank. He had no idea how to exist outside it. He couldn't go back to the university, not if this "experiment" was discovered.

He could no longer deny he was at the end of his rope, and the end was a hangman's noose. Self-pity coursed through his veins as he realized for the first time that his life would be nothing without her.

Thirty days. The only real solution to his problem was unthinkable --- he could release Mara to the sea. No one would ever know she had existed. Perhaps Sony would find her. If so, she might have a chance at survival. If not, then she would adapt or die, like everyone else. But could he bring himself to take that chance?

He sat by the pool until the dome's ominous orange glow marked the setting sun, and he got to his feet.

No more procrastinating. He would get her to Mexico, to Baja California, with its miles of unpopulated shoreline. There he would find a cove in the warm gulf waters. He had connections in Mexico, and might even turn the project over to them, as long as he remained in charge. Authorities across the border had no legal obligation to investigate her circumstances, but they might recognize and reward her value to scientific advancement. Yes, Mexico was the answer. No more procrastinating.

# 17

Mara leaps a rainbow arch as Francisco descends the ladder. The light around him shimmers violet. Her heart feels warm, though the morning is still cold and shadowed.

In one hand he holds a woven bag, in bright colors. She shivers with curiosity. What would come from it this time? Bits of fish, not right from the water, but dry and oiled? Bright red globes exploding with sweetness in her mouth? Cold, dazzling cubes floating, turning into water, disappearing? Buttery rich sweet something he calls ca co ah.

Baring wide flat teeth, bone white against his dark skin, he points at himself. "Fran sees ko," he says, and repeats the sound again. He reaches into the bag and tosses a red globe high. She soars out of the water, catches it, takes it to her island, bites it, then throws it up in the air and catches it again before taking another bite.

He laughs. She likes the sound of this, the only one he makes that is like her own. She understands the deep belly push of air that forces the unexpected sound, as if something inside is leaping for the sky.

She paddles closer, raises herself half out of the pool, sniffing his hands, his arms, with their coat of fine black hairs. He brings an array of new odors. Smoke, rope, and a sweet scent, like flowers. When he leans toward her, she puts her palm in front of his mouth. "On-yon" he says. She hears the "no" sound, falls back into the water, feeling scolded.

From the bright bag he takes a small silver box. She flashes to the edge of the pool, reaching for it. He shakes his head, turns it in his hand many times, light glinting off its surface. The box sings, delicate glassy sounds, like wind chimes, only more measured. It reminds her of the broken red box now at the bottom of the pool, but this song evokes images of spinning suns, stars woven into flexing bands of silver. She tilts her head to better hear the dancing sounds climb, balance, fall, and rise again.

"Moo-see-ka," he repeats over and over, the "see" hissing through his teeth bones. She imitates --- moo-see-ka --- rounding her mouth, stretching her lips, tightening her throat. When her sounds match his, he bares his teeth in something like Sony's smile, and sets the box on the edge of the pool.

She lifts herself onto the ledge, takes the cold dry box in her hands, and pulls it open. No spinning stars, only something cold turning round and round. She closes the box, puts her ear against it, feels rhythmic patterns through her skull bones.

She looks up at the land being, showing her own teeth bones. His violet colors glow brighter. He reaches around and slides a curved, wooden box off his back, runs his fingers across tight strings. A deep roll echoes from the hole in the wood. Patterns of sound match, the way fish scales match. She moves closer, removes her finger fins, pulls on a string with a wet finger. A dull thump. She does not have the thin flat bones on the ends of her fingers to make the moo-see-ka.

He sings, high and fine as early sun, deep as the shadows in the depths of the pool. His colors change along with the flow of sounds, blue, violet, red, purple, the way sun sometimes plays on water.

She raises her head, thickens her throat, tucks in her chin, and imitates him. A low gargle. He laughs. She ducks under the water and flashes away.

Hesitantly, she ripples her body back across the pool and reaches for the wooden box. She grasps his wrist, startled at the force roaring like a waterfall beneath his thin skin, not muffled like Sony's or hers.

His skin is hot and dry. Urgently, she splashes cold water on him, the fins on her hands falling open. He draws back. He does not like water. Perhaps that is why he does not come into the pool, but kneels on the hard concrete, fixed and awkward.

She draws herself up on the side of the pool beside him. His colors flicker, sputter. She tilts her head and strokes the soft place under his chin, like she does for Sony. To her surprise, this land being is not pleased. The colors emanating from him are tinged with yellow, and he stiffens with fear. She does not understand.

She takes his hand, places it against her wet cheek, thinking of Sony, wanting to tell him about Sony. Great waves fill her mind, crescents of white froth. Sony and many other Sony's move as one through green depths, through golden plants taller than the dome, swaying in shafts of light. Clouds of colorful fish move like flocks of birds now move above the dome.

Something beyond the wall rattles. Light is flooding the dome. She knows he is leaving. She makes no-no-no sounds and slaps her finned hands wide on the surface of the water. He speaks softly, finger against lips, and climbs the ladder, taking the bag and the moo see ka. Then he is gone, like Sony.

She swims aimlessly, back and forth across the pool, wondering if Fran-sees-ko will come again, bringing the wooden box with the strings that make wavy music when he runs his fingers across them.

She wonders where Franseesko comes from? She wonders why Waller comes by day through the doors, Franseesko at night, down metal steps, down from the dome, down through the leafy tree. Does he live in the sky?

Maybe one day, like Baby Burrt, like Cranky Duck, like Sony, he will simply not be. Sony went Outside, and did not come back. Franseesko is Outside.

Outside. What would that be? Another dome like this one, always day following night and then another day? Always a land being bringing food and water? Maybe not. Maybe a place where she would be strapped down and pulled from the water, like Sony.

She drops to the bottom of the pool and lies there, barely moving her arms and legs, unwilling to exert the energy to propel herself to the surface, to fill her lungs, to grasp at life. Franseesko is outside. Sony is outside. Outside is.

~ ~ ~ ~

Resolved, Waller said aloud. No more procrastinating. A single call to an old colleague would start the wheels turning.

There was much to be done. He would have to put Mara on intravenous feedings until she would eat on her own, which meant restraining her in the glass tank that she hated. Then, to get her into the tanker, he'd have to shoot her with tranquilizers, and he could not be certain how safe that was. The dart from the gun would be painful in itself, and even a slight miscalculation in dosage could kill her.

He stood looking around the lab, at the tanks of fish, the old coelacanth making its way up a submerged manzanita branch, Octo raising his big head, flipping a tentacle over the edge of his tank as if asking, "What's going on?"

Yes, he would get her to Mexico, but first, he had to get rid of the other animals. The octopus he could sell in San Diego. On the black market, he was worth big money. The coelacanth was worth even more. He hated to part with Octo, but it had to be done.

With dismay, he surveyed the cluttered laboratory, crowded with the results of years of procrastination or parsimony. *One never knew when one might need that bit of inner tube, or that yard of canvas, or that piece of plumbing.* He smiled, remembering something Dolores once said – *a rolling pin gathers no moss.* Well, he had certainly accumulated more than his share of moss. Now that he had to dig out from under it and get rolling, he was appalled.

He surveyed the filing cabinets, rows of them containing all his professional papers, the residue of his early theories and experiments. Where to begin?

Overwhelmed, he went into his room and sank down on the bed, pushing aside a piece of crumpled paper. Oh, yes. An invitation to speak at a seminar. Someone still remembered who he used to be. One of those pseudo-science gatherings in San Diego. "We can reach into the vast inner space of our eternal non-local mind, which transcends both time and space . . ." Non-local mind, he scoffed, crumpling it up again and throwing it on the floor.

He'd gone once. They promised to demonstrate proof for what they called PSI -- Parapsychological theories behind Extrasensory Perception -- Out-of-Body experience, telepathy, precognition, remote viewing, all that nonsense. He had actually sat in their so-called Psi booth with the other suckers and couldn't do any of it. "You have to believe it before you can see it," they claimed. *How's that for tautological reasoning*?

He reached for the box of research articles he'd published years ago, speculating on why dolphins had returned to the sea, eons after their life on land. He couldn't leave those behind.

Back in the lab, he reached for the Scotch, and feeling calmer, pulled the logbook, the record of Mara's existence, from the bottom desk drawer. Wherever she went, with him or without him, it must go with her. Leafing through the pages, he was soon caught in memories - - the challenges and joys of her life. His eyelids were drooping when he put the logbook back in the bottom drawer and locked it.

~ ~ ~ ~

Taking off her lab apron and hanging it by the door, Dolores, eyes wide, told Francisco the professor was preparing to take the coelacanth to San Diego. "I think they give him lots of money, for he say he will pay us when he get back."

Francisco, washing up at the kitchen sink, turned. "What is going on? Why now is he getting rid of everything?"

"*No se.* I ask him, is he living? What about our jobs, I ask him. He just say, don' worry. Then he say a funny thing, Francisco. He say, *If anything happen to me, this old resort goes to you, Dolores.* He look at me, this twisty smile, give me chills. What he think happen to him?"

Francisco, fearing to betray what he knew, said little. He wondered if the old man knew his secret had been discovered. If so, was he going to run? Turn himself in? Or what?

Dolores put a kettle on the front burner. "Maybe he is sick, maybe dying. Back and forth he walks, always so stooped. He look so tired, circles under his eyes like *bolsas*, little purses."

Finally she said, almost reluctantly, "That big jar-like thing? He ask me to clean it. I tole him the hose all rotten. He say don't need those, only the jar."

Francisco's worst fantasies flared. "What does he want it for?"

Dolores shrugged. "It is for sure too small for no big dolphin."

~ ~ ~ ~

Francisco was elated as he put away the ladder late that night. Such progress in so little time. Just a signal, a whistle or a bit song, and she was waiting for him on her island. She was eating now, a little bread last time, though she made a dry face as she tried to swallow it, and dipped it in the pool. Tonight he'd given her a paper cup of bright red jello; she laughed when it wriggled around on her tongue, but she ate all of it.

He must teach her to be quiet, though. When he showed her a small mirror, she laughed loudly at her reflection. And her singing could get them in trouble. Tonight, he feared every moment that something might bring El Professor. He could not keep his night visits a secret much longer. Inevitably the girl would laugh too loudly, or he would leave some telltale clue. He should lay low for a while.

He found the child deeply touching, her purity, the way the light seemed to shine through her, like sun through snow. Even her scars aroused great tenderness in him, the iridescent purple that shadowed her hollowed eyes. Her touch burned his arm still, like dry ice.

Her eyes haunted him. Only in the eyes of children had he seen such an unselfconscious gaze. She had the purity of a primitive, a piece of sculpture, of something that is all self, or no self.

She would be grief stricken if he abandoned her. She had almost died when she lost the dolphin, and was only now beginning to trust again. Since Waller frightened her, she was completely dependent on him, Francisco, a dependence so total as to require nothing whatever in return, no subservience, no pleasing, no striving. Perhaps, he thought, looking at the sky, already pink with dawn, that is our ideal relation to *Los Dios,* the gods.

As he went about repairing another drain spout, making it strong enough to carry his weight should he need to slide down it sometime, he felt an ever-present anger with the man who had done this to her. He should report Waller to the authorities, no matter that he, himself, would be sent back to that filthy prison. But whoever he notified, police or social agency, they would thank him for bringing them the strange captive creature and dismiss him --- Francisco --- the only human she was not afraid of.

He remembered going with Rodrigo once to a sanitarium for the severely disabled, a place where the hard-to-look-at results of genetic failures or medical blunders were hidden away. Scenes from Dante's Inferno, with added stench and din. Seemingly inhuman humans, some with huge misshapen heads, lay in cribs, listless. Others, with mere flippers for arms and legs, crawled about on the filthy floor. A baby a few days old clung to her own tail, several inches long.

"People would be shocked to know how many are born like this," Rodrigo had commented, with a peculiar grin, as if he were embarrassed by nature's failures.

Francisco could never allow her to go to such a place. He yearned to kidnap her, just take her away, but he would have to know first how to care for her. If only he had the logbook Dolores told him about.

"Francisco!" Waller called from the front courtyard. Dolores rescued him, answering him from her window. "He is gone to town." Francisco watched from above as El Doctor went inside.

Dolores was right; the old boy didn't look well lately. He seemed preoccupied, hardly speaking to either of them, holed up in the lab, hour after hour. Francisco was haunted by the thought of that glass laboratory jar, tubes twisting from it like snakes. Dolores said it was in readiness. Ready for what? What was Waller going to do? And when?

# 18

## ~~~~~ FANTASIES ~~~~~

Dolores worked a deep-rooted weed out of her prize cabbages and thinned a row of lacy young carrots. Left to crowd one another, none would be fat and sweet. The garden made her worries seem less real. Francisco's ramblings had become nightly. Always he went to the domed enclosure. Once, she found the ladder against the wall and moved it before El Doctor could see it. She put it back, and didn't tell Francisco. She knew he wasn't in town the morning Waller almost caught him.

If he ever caught her spying on him he would leave. After all, he was only here because he thought he had nowhere else to go, but a man like Francisco, he could go anywhere and people would want him. Women especially.

Maybe Dr. Waller was hiding a beautiful daughter with long golden hair, like in the fairy tales. She had asked him once if he had children; she had found baby bottles, rubber nipples cracked with age. He looked at her in that startled way, as if she had interrupted his inner silence. He said he had used them to feed a young dolphin. She would have thought no more of it, except he went on and on about having a pair of them once, and the female had died. If the female had died, then how did he get a baby dolphin? That alone made her think he wanted to convince her of some lie.

The Tijuana paper once told of a man who kept his thirteen-year-old daughter locked in her room for years. When the police found her, she was like a retarded six year old. Another time, the papers told about a man so jealous he kept his mistress locked up in his apartment while he was at work. The woman lowered herself by a rope each day to be with her family. When he found out, he killed her. Maybe El Doctor was keeping a lunatic wife, or maybe there had been a deformed baby resembling a frog; she saw that in the Tijuana paper also.

Such fantasies, she scolded herself. She had seen many times Dr. Waller take fish from the lab, half dozen or so small ones, swimming live in a bucket, hardly what one would feed a wife, even a lunatic one.

Something had happened. He was more secretive than ever, more moody. The coelacanth was gone, and he paid them as he said he would. Most of the other tanks were empty too. Each day, he looked more and more tired, like a man who doesn't sleep.

Did Francisco have anything to do with that? Sometimes he took from her house little trifles, a mirror, a music box, sweets that she herself had baked for him. For another woman? The thought made her angry, even though he brought most things back. He had looked so guilty when she asked him where he went at night, what else could it be except a woman?

Like a fool, she had cried and begged him to tell her if there was another woman. Every smart girl on *Dias de La Vida* could have told her never to do that. To cry and beg only makes a man feel guilty. Even her grandmother told her, "If he does not see the treasure you are, let him go."

*Something* was wrong. He used to drive her crazy with questions about dolphins, then suddenly he asked no more, except about the log book. Every day he pestered her about that, always making her feel like he would have found it if he were allowed in the lab.

She wished she could be more like her grandmother, who just *knew* things. *Pues*, she would do what Francisco asked. Leave it to him, the man. With the spade, she knocked the dirt off her shoes and went to clean the lab.

Dr. Waller was sorting things into boxes. No use to ask him why. None of her beeswax. He barely glanced up when she passed, going to the kitchen. As she was cleaning spilled fish drippings from the bottom of the refrigerator, she saw him pick up the heavy green book, the logbook, the one he wrote in every day. As if making a decision, he hesitated, then put it in a box with other books and set it aside. She watched him fill another box with canned goods and some packaged food and carry it out to the tanker.

Quickly, hands trembling, she took the logbook, leaving an old phone book in its place, put it with her cleaning supplies and covered it with a towel. She would return it after Francisco read it. That at last would make Francisco happy.

~ ~ ~ ~

Even though her skull is drying like a rapidly tightening clamp, Mara waits on the island. Franseesko brought hope, life, something to live for, like Baba Burrt, Bluebird and Duck. But he has not come down the ladder for three nights and he is not coming now.

She drops to the bottom of the pool. Into the void of her mind, as if through miles of water, comes an indistinct consciousness of Sony. For an instant, she picks up his images: a rush of boundless water, teeming with scents and soundings, with kelp and sea life and coral and exhilarating drafts, ice cold then sensually warm. The images grow stronger. Sony's energy becomes hers. Through his eyes she sees dazzling light far far above, bottomless dark below. All of it begins to spin.

Sony is! She knows he is whirling, spinning, water flying, a thousand diamond prisms catching rainbow sun.

Pushing against her fins, she thrusts to the surface, tilts her head toward the open doors, and hears a faint pulsing, a repeated signal. It is gone as Waller, arms full of tools, hoses and detergent bottles, comes in and starts to dismantle her cove. She swims to the end of the pool, closer to the wooden doors. The vibrations are faint, but clear. It is! It is Sony! Sony calls!

She races around the pool, splashing, leaping chortling, clacking. Sony is! Sony is! Round and round she races, splashing Waller, knocking over feed trays as she dives and surfaces, soaring out of the water as if she could reach the dome.

Waller runs along the edge of the pool, scolding, shouting, "What is the matter with you?"

Eying the open doors, she scrambles out of the pool, falls, pushes to her feet again, falls. Waller shouts, "Stop that. You'll hurt yourself." His words mean nothing.

She is almost to the doors when he gets there first and slams them shut. Sony Sonar signals no more. Waller stands over her, sides heaving, arms akimbo. "What has come over you?"

He lifts her, carries her, protesting, back to the pool, muttering words she does not understand. He responds not at all as she tries to tell him, with clicks and clacks, watery shrieks, and mind pictures, that Sony is, and she must go to him.

"You stay there," Waller scolds as he carries a box of her gear out the gates, closing them firmly behind him. She hears the metal click.

Quietly, making no waves, she crawls out of the pool, crawls and falls across concrete and grass, places her cheek and palms against the wooden planks, listening.

Sony is! Sony is!

~ ~ ~ ~

# 19

## ~~~~~ HEROICS ~~~~~

Waller finally had to send Dolores home. She had taken the old commercial stove apart, cleaned the grease off the interior, the burners, the spill pans, and put it back together again. It looked as though she was never leaving.

"Go on home now. Go on."

She gave him a nervous look, but then she always acted as though he were somehow threatening. Perhaps it was his secretiveness, his academic titles, his size, he didn't know. Preoccupied, not thinking at all clearly, he just wanted her out. He expected a return call from Mexico any minute.

She gathered up her cleaning solvents, and put them in a plastic tub. Still she hovered, as if unsure of something.

"Don't worry about anything you hear tonight," he told her. "Dolphins make very strange noises sometimes."

"But you took the dolphin away," she said, wide eyed.

"There was another dolphin," Waller said, irritated. "Didn't you know that?" He knew there were many clues showing otherwise, but she had never shown that kind of interest.

Deliberately, he laid the tranquilizer gun on the enameled table. Dolores's eyes widened.

"Shoots darts. Tranquilizers." She left, casting a nervous glance at the table. No need to tell her that he'd taken to carrying a real gun under his lab coat.

By the time the dealer finally called, it was well past dark. A reliable buyer had been found, a wealthy entertainment magnate who recognized the value of what Waller was offering and would pay more than Waller ever dreamed. A former scientist himself, the buyer promised appropriate care for the girl and guaranteed publication of Waller's work. No questions asked. They talked big money.

"But you're going to have to get her across the border yourself," the intermediary said. They would pay for the added risk.

Waller agreed to the terms and the deal was sealed. Why was he feeling so desolate? He got what he wanted, didn't he? He poured another Scotch, hands shaking as he set the bottle down.

Because time was running out, he would have to find a safe situation for her in Baja, where the water was warm, while the buyer made arrangements, which could take time. He couldn't wait around here with that fool Mexican on the loose.

He faced the empty fish tanks, forlorn as abandoned houses. Octo, grumpy and querulous, thrashed his many arms, seeming to know he was the only one left, clouding the water with ink.

For years the octopus, the old coelacanth, and the dolphins were all the family Waller had. And now, losing the girl.... A jet plane droned overhead, its great engines chewing into the black night sky. He felt as if he were on the bottom of the ocean, the plane churning the surface like a boat.

He was tired to the point of dizziness, but he could not rest. For days, Mara had eaten nothing. That meant strapping her into the sterile glass tank for intravenous feeding, and the only way he would ever get her into that tank was thoroughly tranquilized.

Turning out the lights, he waited in darkness by the pool doors, gripping the loaded tranquilizer gun, hoping to get a good shot.

~ ~ ~ ~

As Francisco lifted the heavy glass pane, he worried that the girl would not be waiting as she usually was. He had heard nothing from the pool all day. Maybe El Doctor had already taken her away. Perhaps she was already fastened in the glass tank, tortured like some miserable victim of the inquisition. No. Looking down on the parking lot, he saw the tanker, haphazard boxes of supplies and equipment heaped around it.

He laid the glass aside, and there she was, lying on the island below, listless. As soon as she saw him, she dove into the water, came back up, and with remarkably swift kicking of her lower legs, held herself out of the water from the waist up, clapping soundlessly as a seal. As he came down the ladder, she swam circles of excitement.

Kneeling at the pool, he shushed her, and she imitated the gesture, putting a webbed finger over her lips, making her eyes big. He laughed softly and held out one of Dolores's empanadas, buttery, filled with honey. He took her hand and dried the fins on his shirt so the pastry would not get soggy.

She ate the sweet pastry without dipping it into water as she usually did, and held her palm out to him, sticky with honey. It was such an endearing gesture, he took her hand and kissed it.

~ ~ ~ ~

The tranq gun seemed almost to pull Waller through the doors. Quiet. Quiet. He stood there, dumbfounded. By the light of the green underwater globe, he saw the kneeling Mexican holding the girl's hand to his lips! She, who would never allow Waller to even touch her!

With a roar, he charged, tranq gun ready.

Mara, clacking and shrieking, plunged into the pool and raced to safety behind the mermaid.

As Francisco sprinted for the ladder, Waller fired. The dart whanged into the ladder, and careened off. Francisco whirled, reversed direction, and ducked out through the doors, Waller after him.

~ ~ ~ ~

Slamming the courtyard doors, Francisco jammed a stick between the curved handles and sprinted around the building. He heard the older man thud into the gates, once, twice, then the stick snapped and heavy footfalls pounded across the front drive.

He headed for the woods, falling over a down branch, tumbling into the brushy canyon. Leaping to his feet, he plunged on, manzanita dragging at his clothes, yucca spikes ripping at his ankles.

Sliding into the shadow of a huge boulder, he quieted his breathing, cursing the lantern moon that threw its light across the open slope ahead. He could hear Waller coming closer, thrashing about in the bushes.

Carefully, he fumbled about on the ground and found a stone the size of his fist, sharp on one side, round and smooth in his palm. Every muscle tense to strike, he waited. In the distance, a mourning dove called its endless existential question. High above, a jet surged ahead, its lights blinking white lanes through midnight blue.

The old man was combing the slope, coming closer, then away, closer, then away. Francisco pressed his back into the shadows.

Suddenly Waller's silhouette loomed in front of him, back turned, pistol ready.

Francisco lifted the rock. Power surged through his arm.

Before he could bring himself to strike, Waller plunged forward, slipping and sliding on the steep slope, head and shoulders disappearing behind a twisted black oak. Francisco sagged back against the boulder, feeling like his Adams apple had a knife through it. His legs trembled. He wiped sweat from his eyes. He had almost killed his second man.

He hurled the stone as far as he could, far down into the canyon's dark shadows, where it crashed with a hollow *thunk* into a tree. As Waller pursued that sound, Francisco eased himself up the slope, stealthy as a lizard.

~ ~ ~ ~

Waller sank onto the concrete bench in front of the laboratory, his belly heaving. He hadn't realized how badly out of shape he had become over the years. With a torn sleeve he wiped blood off his forehead where a sharp limb had given him a bad gash.

Damned interfering Mexican. So now the child was turning to Francisco instead of to him. No wonder he, Waller, had gotten nowhere with her. Next time it would not be a tranq gun! Damned Mexican.

Hearing someone behind him, he jumped to his feet. Dolores appeared from the darkness, clutching her nylon robe to her chest. Anxiously she surveyed the tangled canyon. "You see my husband?"

"No. Not tonight." How much did she know? He wondered. Had her husband told her about the girl in the pool?

She drew herself up to full height, a determined set to her young face. "Dr. Waller, something strange goes about here."

"Strange? What do you mean?"

"I think you keep a woman ... a woman in there?" She gestured toward the dome, a greenish glow above the lighted pool.

Waller laughed, a scornful snort. "A woman! Absurd."

"Francisco, always he gets up in the night. Sometimes he take things, sweets, trinkets . . ."

Ah. So that was it. "What's he up to?"

"*No se.*" She looked down, her small hand tracing the patterned flowers on her robe. Then she looked at him directly. "I think maybe you know."

He stood speechless. This young woman stood before him, hair tousled from sleep, chin up, gently challenging him. Each night she must have lain there thinking there was another woman, yet here she was, scouring the canyon, worried for her husband. There was more courage and dignity about her than Waller had recognized before. If he could tell her the truth, it would put her mind at ease. Instead he said, "If he has a woman, I know nothing of it. Since he has you, I doubt it." He felt foolish and awkward mouthing such flattery. Still, it was true.

Scanning the canyon, she huddled into her robe. The moon accented black, twisted shadows. A mist was blowing in off the ocean, scuttling like a luminous ghost toward them. A forbidding place, still she went sliding down the embankment, looking for Francisco.

~ ~ ~ ~

Mara lies behind the copper mermaid, shaking uncontrollably. The violence of the two men terrifies her, seems to taint the very air. She watches the doors, ready to dive into the deep end of the pool if either returns. She stares at the place where Bluebird used to come and go, wishing she could make herself that small.

Sony is. That she knows. She lifts her head and warbles high sharp calls. Sound careens off the dome, leaving only hollow echoes.

In the dim glow of the pool light, she eyes the metal steps. She edges her way across the grass, her eyes following the steps into the branches, and eases her weight onto the first rung. If her tender feet can bear the bruising pain, she can do this. She takes another step, and another, until she is in the avocado branches.

Looking down, she is dizzy at the thought of falling through air, no water to catch her, only hard ground. Or worse, cement. She steels herself and moves another step upward. The ladder shakes. A branch blocks her forearm. She grabs. The branch snaps, sending the ladder hurtling backward.

This she knows how to do. Her legs double, her feet thrust hard. She dives into the pool.

~ ~ ~ ~

# PART IV

~~~~~~

## REVELATIONS

~~~~~~~~~~

# 20

## ~~~~~ TURNABOUT ~~~~~

Francisco circled up the hill behind the lab, got his bike from the shed, a canteen of water, a package of corn chips, and a hammer that happened to be lying on the floor. The hammer was the only weapon he had, except for a pocketknife too small to do any real damage. He had no idea what to do next. He could not go back to the pool without getting caught, nor could he just abandon that surreal and beautifully innocent child.

With only the moon to go by, and that obscured by clouds coming in off the ocean, he pushed his bicycle through the eucalyptus. On the road, he waited out of sight a few minutes to see if anyone had come looking for him, trying to think without all the adrenalin interfering.

He felt suddenly very alone, knowing that whatever happened now, he would have to leave, either with or without the dolphin girl, with or without Dolores. He would have to leave just when he had become almost at home in these hills, with their windy and wild view of the ocean. Almost at home with Dolores and her cranky boss. Almost at home, fixing things, keeping things working. Too late now to think about that.

What to do? He circled downhill. Half a mile below the lab, there was a hairpin turn and a large concrete drainage pipe big enough to hide out in. If Waller tried to leave covertly, taking the girl with him, he would have to take the tanker over this road, then take the coast road to the freeway.

Francisco would hear the big engine in plenty of time to position himself on the bank above the hairpin turn, then drop onto the truck as Waller slowed down. This time, he would have the element of surprise on his side.

~~~~

"I am a nervous wrack," Dolores muttered. Francisco's bicycle was gone from the shed. His blankets too, and the daypack they used for their picnics. With a flashlight, she followed bicycle tracks.

She had not been worried about Francisco's safety until Waller sent her home. He had laid the heavy gun-like thing on the metal table with a clang, so deliberately, so obviously, that she knew he wanted to frighten her, to keep her away. Later, there was all the noise, yelling, running feet.

El Doctor said he knew nothing of Francisco, had not seen him, but she knew he was lying. She had seen the gash on his head, the dirt on his pants, the manzanita twig under his shoelace. He had pulled his lab coat tight to cover what might have been a gun. He even tried to sweet talk her. That was not like him. Francisco was onto something, and Dr. Waller knew it.

Until Francisco got mixed up in it, she never thought about the professor's work. She never expected to understand it anyway, the books and papers he was always reading. Francisco said he was evil, but she could not believe that. Even though he was gruff with her, he spent many hours taking care of his fishes, making sure their tanks were clean, their water fresh, their food just right.

Especially the octopus. El Professor spent many hours with that ugly one. She had seen him put his hand in the tank, letting the creepy tentacles wrap around his arm. He smiled then the way mothers do when babies clutch their fingers. She saw his face when he said he was going to take the octopus away. It reminded her of the day her brother accidentally ran over his own cat. An octopus is a strange thing to grieve over, but El Doctor was a man who liked wet swimmy things. He was just like that. She never questioned.

The bicycle tracks disappeared in the woods. She stood in the dusty road, stymied.

What happened with Francisco? Where was he? Maybe headed back to Mexico and his precious Bianca. Her throat choked up at the thought. How could he leave like that so suddenly, without a word? Then she was angry. Did he care so little? If he was on his way to Mexico, to Bianca, what did she care about him?

Maybe Francisco was not gone at all; maybe there was something both he and the Doctor were in cahoots about. She could not make tales or heads of it. After all, was she a big-shot detector?

The logbook she had stolen for Francisco. It would have the answers.

Hurrying back to her casita, she took the logbook out of the bucket of cleaning supplies, still wrapped in a towel. With only a twinge of guilt, she put it on the kitchen table, sat down and opened the battered, water marked cover. Reading had never been easy for her, and Waller's scrawling penmanship didn't help. She could make no odds and ends of it.

Gradually she realized the words were not English, or Spanish either, but some other language. Well, if she could read none of it, it would be no use to Francisco either.

She wrapped it in the towel and carried it back to the lab, making sure Waller was out in front before quietly entering by the back door. In the lab's dim light, the octopus waved his smarmy arms while she put the logbook where it belonged, in the bottom drawer of the desk, and turned the key. Maybe, seeing it there, El Doctor would think he himself left it, he was so turvy-topsy lately. She put the key on the top of the desk where he would be sure to find it, and tiptoed out.

~ ~ ~ ~

Waller had to work quickly now, had to get the girl out of there before the fool Mexican came back with the authorities. What a vision that brought! They would jail the mad scientist! Crowds would bring their children to see the webbed wonder girl!

He put his loaded pistol in the pocket of his lab coat and picked up the tranq gun. He would be ready this time. Through the big double doors, he saw the girl sprawled on the rock island. The ladder lay nearby. My God! Had she tried to escape? When he approached, she gave a frightened cry and dropped into the deep water on the far side of the pool.

Anger flared anew. He had cared for her all her life, even created that life, had sacrificed everything for her, yet she despised him. That Mexican could kiss her hand, but she would rather die or run away than let Waller touch her.

He edged along the pool. A sardine floated on the surface of the murky water, belly up. He had not found time to change the water in days. Francisco could add that to his horror story --- a starved child in a filthy pool.

He banged the wooden doors open and shut. She would think he'd gone back inside. Then he lay down flat in the grass, tranq gun braced, and waited. Got to get it right; hitting her in the wrong place could be fatal.

Finally, she crawled onto the island, her form clearly silhouetted. His knuckles loomed large on the tranq gun, as if the whole world had come to rest there. Bracing his quaking wrist with his other hand, he started to squeeze the trigger, but she moved. What was she doing? He watched with amazement. She was eating an avocado, spitting out the bitter skin and biting into the soft, tasty fruit inside.

She had somehow gotten herself across the grass to the avocado tree, a distance of several yards, and picked an avocado. She was eating! This made things easier. No need for a tranquilizer.

No need to strap her into the glass tank. No hated intravenous feedings. He could slip her into the tanker and get out of here now, tonight, before that interfering Mexican told anyone what he had seen - - not that anyone would believe him. A dolphin girl?

He pulled the lever to start draining the pool so he wouldn't have to use the net to catch her, an impossible task, then he hurried to ready the truck for the trip across the border.

~ ~ ~ ~

Dolores had time now to check the casita. Nothing was gone. Not the tortillas from the breadbox. Not the money from the tea canister over the stove. Now she didn't think Francisco had gone to Mexico. A daypack and a bicycle. You do not travel far that way. You take money, the first thing you think of. Also, his grandfather's watch, his greatest treasure, lay in plain sight on the table by the door. If he had not gone to Mexico, was something worse going on? Was he right, that Waller was evil?

She quelled her morbid fantasies. If Francisco did not come back by morning, she would gather tomatoes from the garden. It always made her feel better to gather tomatoes, or peas, or green beans. Good things. Nourishing. Satisfying. When something terrible happens, her grandmother always said, go right on doing what you would be doing anyway. It brings order back to the world.

She stared out the window at the lab, where lights were blazing. El doctor had slammed that tranquilizer gun on the table, making, as they say, a point. She remembered what Francisco had read to her; a dolphin's breathing is not automatic, but a conscious choice. So if he is tranquilized, wouldn't he drown? Then was the tranquilizer gun meant to be used on Francisco?

Pulling on jeans and a sweater, she took the back way to the lab again, ragged eucalyptus bark crunching underfoot. Feeling her way in the dark, she stumbled on the caved in edge of a dry irrigation ditch and slid down feet first, catching hold of a shred of black plastic as she landed. Her other hand came down on something hard, hairy, and round. She picked it up, knocked off the clogged dirt, and held it at arms length. *Aagggah!* A skull! She dropped it.

A dolphin skull, she thought at first. No. Too small. Too round. The rows of teeth too flat. Cringing, she brushed more dirt away. A few strands of long dirty hair came off in her hand. A shudder went through her. Francisco was right after all. Some kind of horror had been going on here.

Until then, she had not wanted to go for the police. They would send Francisco back to Mexico, arrest him even. But now he might be in worse danger. She dared not go in the lab to use the phone. Waller was there. She got her bicycle and headed down the front drive to the paved road, not caring whether he saw her or not. She would find a policeman at the Junction Diner, where the cops always had coffee.

# 21

## ~~~~~ SEVERED LINES ~~~~~

Francisco must have fled, Waller decided. Why else would Dolores have taken off on her bicycle, except to look for him? Still, he felt uneasy. Evidently the Mexican had not called the police or they would have been here by now, but there was no way to know for sure. There were just too many uncertainties, too many variables. Circumstances were forcing him to do quickly what he would have had to do eventually --- get her out of here.

He trusted the dealer, had ties with him from his University days, but so many things could go wrong --- a border guard more alert and honest than usual, an underhanded buyer, a Mexican double-cross. Anything was possible where the black market and that much money were involved.

He felt disoriented, almost ill. It had always been his nature to move slowly, and for many years he had been able to set his own pace. Now he stood before a closet jammed with clothing; suits and ties from his professorial days, even his baccalaureate gown, shoulders dust laden. He would need a suit, even an outdated one, to establish credibility, so he pried one off a crowded hanger. He knelt by an array of polished leather shoes, unable to make even this simple decision. Most had not been worn in years, and would make his feet hurt. A pair of Nikes went on the bed with the suit. Then a dress shirt, not quite as white as it once was.

Boxes of food and outmoded camping gear already filled the entire space behind the seat of the truck, and he still had to pack all Mara's necessities. Her needs were not simple: a complete medical kit, water purifiers, a specially adapted bidet. Those he heaped into the passenger side of the truck, along with tarps, wraps, blankets and a flashlight. Almost ready.

But what if something went wrong? He went back to the lab and gathered gages, tanks, heaters, anything he might possibly need. When he crammed the last boxes in the cab, there was no room for Octo's tank, and the octopus could not possibly go into the tanker with the girl.

Back in the lab he stood looking at Octo's tank. The big head emerged, a tentacle whipped out of the water and flung one of Dolores' wooden kitchen tools at him. "All right. All right, old friend." One last time he fed the sprawling beast some oysters, then scrawled a note: *Dolores, take care of Octo until I get back.* Already old for an octopus, he probably wouldn't live much longer anyway. Leaving a long list of instructions, Waller added, *When you change his water, talk to him, he likes that.*

If Francisco was bringing the authorities, they could be here any time, and the worst job was yet to be done. Mara.

He leaned against the doorway, exhausted, desperate for sleep, his back aching, fighting the urge to just put everything back where it was. He cursed Francisco's guile, his swiftness, his agile good health. The heat of his rage propelled him back into action.

After downing the last of the Scotch and filling a dish with fresh shrimp, Mara's favorite delicacy, he went to the pool. It should be almost empty by now.

Damn. The water level was only a little lower than it was when he first opened the drain. Clogged. That would make things a lot more difficult. He grabbed the net, knowing she was probably behind the mermaid, pressed close against the stone banks of the island.

"Come on, Mara. Come on! No playing around tonight. We've got to get going." He tossed a large pink shrimp onto the island, but she refused to show herself. He tossed another into the deep water, where she might feel safer. Nothing.

"Okay, we do it the hard way." He switched on the bright overheads, which always made her edgy, but now he could see her in the deepest part of the pool, undulating only enough to hold her position. With grim determination, he grasped the net's long handle, circled around behind her, and quickly brought it down. But Mara was no fish. She pushed the hoop off, nearly yanking him into the water, then threw herself onto the island, and raising her head, cried out in bird-like shrieks, more like a seagull than a human being.

"Sony's gone. You can stop that," Waller growled. Wading into the shallow end of the pool, he lunged. The edge of the hoop hit her hip, leaving long red streaks as she dodged.

Terrified, shrieking, she raced in circles around the pool, quick as a silverfish, and hovered at the deep end, watching his every movement.

He lunged, slipped on wet tiles and fell, badly turning his knee. Grimacing with pain, furious, he saw she was back behind the island again.

He would have to be cruel to be efficient. He went for the contraption he'd designed when he was training Sony, a long net fastened on a rod the width of the pool. He would be in over his head, but he'd solved that, too, working with dolphins years ago.

In the shed he found his old scuba equipment, tested the hoses, the regulator, the mask, the vest, found the weights he'd cobbled together, and carried it all out to the pool. Tossing the tranq gun in a heap with his clothes, he strapped on the vest and tank, stepped into the weights and laced them tight. Wearing only scuba equipment and cotton shorts, he waded in. There was no way she could escape him now.

~ ~ ~ ~

In the dark tunnel of the drainage pipe, Francisco had no way to measure time. Beyond the rim of the culvert he could see only a few tangled trees, bats soaring from limb to limb like small black devils, gathering bugs. He hoped his hideout was not their home; he found their mousy winged bodies repulsive.

Directly above him, the stars seemed very close. Coyotes yipped and yowled in the distance, like lost spirits. He sharpened his pocketknife and hefted the hammer, trying to imagine using it on a human being. He built elaborate rescue plans, ending with the delicate girl clinging to him in gratitude.

If the truck did not come soon, he would know el Doctor was satisfied that he had been scared off, then he would sneak back, tie up the madman, force him to give up the logbook, and one way or another, he would rescue the girl.

When the truck still did not come after what seemed hours, he climbed from his hiding place, stretched his cramped muscles, and started pedaling back uphill.

Rounding the bend, he stopped and left the bicycle in the trees. Every light was on, even the string of outdoor bulbs that ran across the parking lot. The dome glowed like translucent china. The tanker truck was parked in front, facing the road.

Moving slowly, he eased across the parking lot and crouched in a tangle of overgrown bougainvillea next to the walled pool area. If only he had the ladder. The night was quiet except for the sing-song of crickets and occasional rustlings of a squirrel in the canyon. With a rush of wings, an owl flew up from the shadows, its hollow call mocking. Then, a quiet so still it was ominous.

He yearned to whistle some kind of signal, let the girl know she was not alone, but he dared not. Sharply, suddenly, came her high rapid cry, half dolphin, half human. Her danger call.

Heedless of his own safety, Francisco dashed around the building and threw himself against the patio doors. Latched.

Leaping high, he grasped a rusty drainpipe, and started climbing, feeling weightless, driven by something more powerful than adrenalin. A support snapped, but as the drain sagged away from the building, he got a hold on the ledge and pulled himself onto the roof.

The plank was gone. He jumped the two feet to the dome, and ignoring ground glass tearing at his skin, crouched on the ledge and peered through the opening.

Below, in the green glow of the pool lights, he saw confirmation of his worst fantasies --- a grotesque doughy body, naked except for ballooning shorts and scuba gear, moved through the water, pursuing the girl. Through a haze of anger, he saw Waller pushing ahead of him a curtain of netting, forcing the girl into a smaller and smaller space. Soon she would be trapped.

He stared, transfixed. The grotesquerie, totally submerged, moved relentlessly forward, hoses trailing around the bloated form like the arms of an octopus. The girl flashed back and forth in a small, rapidly compressed space.

Throwing himself over the edge, Francisco hung by his fingers from a band of copper, then swinging wide, he dropped, crashing through the branches of the avocado tree, rolling as he hit the ground.

At the pool's edge he leaped to his feet. Waller, unaware of his presence, was slowly, eerily, advancing, like some B-movie astronaut, lines floating laconically around him. The girl, tangled now, trapped in the net, fought desperately to free herself.

Francisco could bear it no longer. With one swift motion, he scooped a long-handled net off the ground, thrust the hoop end into the water, twisted it among the tangled hoses, and jerked them loose. While they spun like snakes in the water, he backed off and waited for the man to surface or drown.

Moments passed. Like a tethered balloon, Waller's bloated figure tumbled and turned, arms groping, trying to free himself from the weights that held him.

It was within Francisco's power to let him drown. Waller had kept a helpless child in this concrete pool; it was fitting he should die there. But Francisco still carried guilt for taking one life. Did he want to murder another, even this less-than-worthless specimen of humanity?

Reaching into the roiling water, he grabbed a twisted hose and towed El Doctor, helpless as a beached whale, to the shallow end of the pool.

The man heaved himself out of the water and onto the tiles, face down, gasping and choking, chest heaving, skin blue. Finally he sat up, looking for what had nearly killed him. When he saw Francisco, one roar expressed all his rage. "You!"

Perhaps out of triumph, or because the situation was so melodramatically absurd, Francisco laughed.

Flushing red, Waller kicked free of the weights, grabbed a sharp, short-handled spade from the weeds and charged, swinging it over his head, coming so fast that Francisco couldn't get the hammer from under his belt. He dove under the shovel, butting his head into the other man's great belly.

As Waller staggered backward, Francisco slipped on the wet tile and went down. Suddenly the red face loomed above him, the spade's sharp pointed edge inches away from his throat. He grabbed it and twisted, hard, but Waller's weight was placed solidly, his grip strong on the handle. Francisco found himself slammed against the wall. Waller faced him from a few feet away, breathing heavily, his glance shifting toward a pile of clothes.

Francisco tugged the hammer free. That moment gave his opponent a slight edge. With a roar, Waller swung the shovel, and the hammer flew. The shovel clanged into the wall. Both men threw themselves after it. Francisco, ripping the handle from the other's grasp, emerged with the shovel, but Waller had the hammer.

Francisco circled, the shovel raised. Waller, fueled by fury, raised the hammer. With a feinting motion, Francisco threw the heavier man off balance, then came in with a downward slash of the shovel, gouging Waller across one forearm. Waller fell, grasping a flap of torn flesh, blood pouring through his fingers.

Francisco stood over him, breathing hard, shovel in one hand, hammer in the other, the figure at his feet shaking with pain and cold.

"What do you want, anyway?" Waller groaned, teeth chattering.

Francisco turned over the heap of clothes with his foot, and seeing no weapon, tossed a shirt to Waller. Waller babbled something in English as he tore off the scuba vest and wrapped his arm in the shirt. Gesturing at the girl with his good arm, he seemed to be trying to tell Francisco something about her, but he spoke so quickly, Francisco couldn't understand. He needed help.

Still keeping an eye on Waller, he worked his way along the wall to the double doors. "Dolores?" No response. "Dolores!" he bawled again.

"She go, she no hear," Waller said in the pidgin English that infuriated Francisco, but the knowledge sobered him. Somewhere in the back of his mind, he had been counting on her.

Feeling like a fool in some low-grade movie, he tied Waller's hands and feet with cords from the weights, using knots he could never untie, while Waller whimpered, "Cold. Frio."

The ocean air blowing in off the coast was indeed frio. "Congratulations." Francisco scoffed. "A lifetime an hour away from Mexico, and you've managed to learn one word of Spanish."

Disdain in his very walk, he went inside for a blanket, came back and draped it over the shivering man.

"Yo---I," he said, pointing at himself. "Will not hurt you. *Pero usted*," he pointed at Waller, "You go to jail for what you have done to that child. You do not touch her, never again. *Comprende?*"

Waller looked up at him, red eyes heavy with hate.

"Where is the book?" Francisco demanded. "The logbook you keep? Los *recuerdos de la nina?*"

Waller looked away. "No *comprende.*" Francisco knew he was lying.

They both looked at the girl hovering at the surface of the water, her hairless skull shining dove-white in the bright overhead lights. "You will never touch her again," Francisco said.

He knelt by the pool, taking her hands in his, feeling as protective and as helpless as he had years ago, when his little nephew, deathly ill, had crawled into his lap, murmuring *Tio*, Uncle.

The girl was shivering violently. Fear, not cold. He ran his finger down her cheek and sang softly, hoping to calm her. "*In sus ojos viven siempre todo el mundo.*" --- In your eyes lives always the whole world. She laid her cheek against his hand, clinging to him. Her trust touched him deeply.

Gently, he disengaged her. "He will never hurt you again."

"I go now to call the police," he told Waller. "To jail you'll go for what you have done to her."

Turning at the gate to make sure Waller stayed put, he saw the girl had gone back under water. All he could see was the net, floating like algae on the surface of the pool.

~ ~ ~ ~

# 22

ILLUMINATIONS ~~~~~

In front of a dusty phone directory, Francisco found the pages printed in Spanish and dialed the number for the Sheriff. While the phone buzzed repeatedly, he wondered what he was going to tell them. That he, an illegal, had beaten and tied up a noted scientist in his own home?

A woman answered, abrupt, already impatient. "Sheriff Department. Yes?"

"*Habla Espanol?*" Francisco asked.

"Si. Poquito." He relaxed, feeling easier.

"I want to report a case of ... child abuse? Wait. Maybe kidnapping, I'm not sure what to call it."

"Your name please?"

He hesitated.

"The victim's name then."

"I don't know her name."

"Can't you ask her? How old is she?"

"Who knows? Maybe three, maybe ten."

"Sir! You must know whether she's three or ten." He could almost hear her mastering her irritation. "Would you put her on the phone please?" He was getting that hopeless feeling he always got when trying to deal with American authorities.

He could hear other phones ringing in the background, other busy voices.

"I can't do that. She isn't ..."

"Do you need an ambulance?"

"No! She is all right ... in that way."

She broke in, her voice sharp. "Look, just bring her on down here."

"No. Someone must come here."

The woman sighed. "I don't know how soon I can get someone. Is there a third party involved?"

"Yes. He is here. Tied up."

There was a pause. "You intend to press charges then."

"No. I cannot stay here."

"Sir, someone has to press charges, or you will have an assault and battery charge on your hands. Now what is the address?"

"Un momento." Francisco set the receiver down.

He would get the official address from El Doctor's wallet. *Americanos* carried wallets with them always. Identification, they called it, as if one's identity were credit cards, insurance numbers and driver's license. He headed for the door, turned the knob. Tried it again. Pushed hard. It was locked!

The phone sent a disconnect signal. In disgust, he yanked the line from the wall, and started for the other door.

Locked.

~ ~ ~ ~

If Waller hadn't fallen on the shard of broken glass, he never would have found it. His wrists burned from sawing through wet cords with it. The cut on his back was probably still bleeding. As he pulled the rest of his clothes from the soggy pile, he found the pistol still in the pocket of his lab coat. A good thing the Mexican was so sure of himself he hadn't checked carefully, a good thing he himself didn't have a chance to use the gun, angry as he was. He didn't really want to kill anybody. He just wanted him out of the way for a few hours.

What could he report to the police anyway? A strange hairless girl held captive in a swimming pool? Such a fantastic story from a Mexican peon, about a respectable professional like himself would not be taken seriously. Still, one could not be sure. He had no choice but to get out as fast as possible, and that meant he had to use the tranquilizer gun. It was the only way now, thanks to the Mexican.

Mara, terrified, was huddled behind the bronze mermaid. He fired off a dart. It careened off the bronze and ricocheted back, falling point down, grazing his own bare foot. The bronze figure seemed to mock him. He took aim again, and the dart pierced her hip. In seconds, she went limp and he hauled her out of the pool, all the fight gone. Wrapping her in clear plastic to protect her from dehydration, he covered her with a blanket and laid her on the seat of the cab.

She was still breathing, thank God. He feared even that mild dosage might have been excessive. There was no time to check her pulse. Francisco was pounding on the door, yelling. "You better leave her alone, Waller! The cops are on the way."

What would they find? Nothing but a peon acting crazy. Waller climbed into the cab, leaned her unconscious form against his shoulder, and started the engine. He would put her in the tank as soon as the tranquilizers wore off. If they caught him, who would look there?

Putting the truck in gear, he took a last look at his home of many years, good years that he hadn't even known were good, years of sunlight on a blue-green pool where the girl and her dolphin played, innocent as puppies. There was no way back.

~ ~ ~ ~

Francisco heard the tanker roar into motion and move away from the building. With all his strength, he hoisted a chair and swung it at the window, breaking through the glass but leaving the wrought iron bars in place. With a broomhandle, he tried to pry them loose from their hold in the stuccoed brick. No luck. "Dolores! Help me! Dolores!" Where was she?

He watched helplessly as the truck's headlights slowly disappeared down the rugged coast road. If they made it to the main highway, he would never again see the girl, never know if she were dead or alive. He could still feel the small hand in his, still see the trust in her eyes as he walked away from her, making promises that he could not keep.

He gave the heavy door another kick, sending him reeling back against the desk, nearly weeping with frustration. Why had he disconnected the phone?

The entire grounds lay in darkness. Waller had pulled the power switch. Where was Dolores? She had told him where the logbook was, and now he, foolish man, was locked up here with a logbook that was of no use to him. He had done it all wrong.

Since there was nothing he could do until Dolores showed up, he found matches, lit the stubs of candles on the back of the desk, and pulled on the bottom drawer. Locked, like she said. When he ran his hands under some papers, searching for a key, his fingers slid across a pool of slimy water. *Yuk.*

Candlelight shone on a trail of slime running up the wall behind the fish tanks. Curious, he followed the splotchy trail. Clutched in one waving tentacle, the octopus held a shiny golden ring, and on it, the treasured key.

~ ~ ~ ~

The back road was never meant for speed. As Waller shifted down for the worst curves and ruts, heaped boxes tumbling against him, he touched the pistol under his waistband, laughing bitterly at the absurdity of it all -- slashing shovels and broken glass. *Am I going a bit crazy?* The dome slowly disappeared from his rearview mirror.

The girl twitched restlessly against his shoulder. If she woke while he was driving, her struggles could get them both killed. He looked for a place to pull over, something out of sight. Spotting some weedy car tracks leading into a grove of large oaks, an unused lover's lane, he parked in the shadows and waited for her to wake, but she only shifted, making incoherent sounds, as animals do in their dreams, and lapsed back into drugged sleep.

While Mara slept on his shoulder, he sat quietly, resting from everything he had been through, listening to the sounds of the night, the singing of crickets, the distant lament of a coyote, the soft stirring of wind in the trees. An overhanging oak hung its black limbs over them like the wings of a nesting hen. A star hung from the moon like a watch fob.

He had not realized until now, in this quietude, how much pain, anxiety and fear he'd been living with. So long without sleep, and then that battle with Francisco, he was more tired than he'd been in his entire life. But he'd bested the s.o.b..

Holding the sleeping child, watching her quiet face, the faint Sony-like smile, he relaxed.

Now that the worst had happened, he quit struggling, surrendered somehow, as the minutes passed. He no longer worried --- what would happen, where would he go, how would he live? He felt as if he'd crossed some kind of line, given over control, passed some point at which it no longer mattered what happened. With nothing left to lose, he no longer felt any fear.

Or was it that brief jolt of the tranquilizer dart, hardly noticed at the time? Whatever the cause, it was a pleasant change. Sheltered by trees, by rounded hills, smooth and soft as seals, he felt content in every pore, every cell, every vessel of his body and soul.

He looked down at the soft defenseless face. Was this the way it was with her before he took Sony away? Unconditional trust, experienced in her body, as well as her mind? She stirred, burrowed into his shoulder, twisted one long webbed foot around the other, and quieted again.

Through the windshield, he could see a shimmer of ocean below the sloping hills. *The ocean from which we all come*, he thought. The sight released in his memory an old song from his school choir. The words came to him as if from outside himself.

> *The Bells of Saint Mary's*
> *Ah, Hear.*
> *They are calling*
> *the young loves the true loves*
> *who come from the sea ...*

Odd, the thoughts that kept coming. They didn't seem quite his own. Images, rather than language, like the time he'd taken psychedelics in an off-campus grad-school experiment.

Who come from the sea. He thought of the old coelacanth. With the thought he *became* the ancient fish, the giant coelacanth, lying on the bottom of the sea. His hands were fins, shoveling bits of earth over the eggs of his mate. His arms were paddles, slow, deliberate, and his stubby rotating legs pushed in dumb intrinsic motion against the ocean floor as he pushed toward land.

Gradually the sense of that ancient creature eased away, followed by another powerful wave. Now he was a lizard, lying on a rock that still held the heat of the sun. His heart beat in the hollow drum of his throat, his separated eyes sharply focused, like two pencil leads, on a fly he was about to lash with his sticky tongue.

Then he was soaring, cutting through air, swinging feathered wing on feathered wing, his lizard eyes scanning for food. He morphed into a furred creature, groundling, hungry, wiry, his jaw huge, jutting around flat teeth, hands, dangling near the ground. He felt the lightness of his consciousness, the clear dignified simplicity of his ape mind.

Fleetingly the words he once jeered at floated past: *We can reach into the vast inner space of our eternal mind, which transcends both time and space.*

Where did it come from, this powerful flood of knowing? Did it exist somewhere within him, released by his weariness? Induced by the tranquilizer? Or was he tapping into the consciousness of the tender creature leaning so heavily against his shoulder?

As he thought of her, a new image filled him with wonder, a young female, small, graceful, very very intelligent in some way he did not fully comprehend, with a sensibility such as he had never known, foreign yet at home in the world, delicate yet strong. He sensed in her a deep certainty, a knowing. Then he *was she*, and knew her longing, her almost unbearable longing, to return to the sea.

He studied her strong body, shaped by years of water. Could Mara, a water being, actually be the next evolutionary step?

Coming back to himself, he took a few minutes to distinguish between physical reality and thought. Only one thing he knew for certain, drawn from those few moments in a trance state: All creation is one being. We are connected to one another within a medium called consciousness, in which all time, all being, is experienced now, all creation evolving together.

Mara stirred, restless. Her eyes opened, fixed on him for a second, then wandered. In a moment she would be unmanageable. He had to get her into the tank while he still could.

Struggling awkwardly to hold on to her, he climbed up the metal ladder, opened the hatch, slid her from the plastic sheath, and she dropped into the water with a splash. He watched her as, revived by cold, she swam from one end of the tanker to the other, back and forth, back and forth, like a caged animal. Shuddering, he closed the hatch.

~ ~ ~ ~

Mara is falling .........falling ..........a stinging blow across her thighs. Startled by cold water, awakened to darkness such as she has never known. Awakened to a blackness so deep, she cringes into herself. So this is Outside.

She throws herself against the darkness, kicks against it, a hollow metal thud. She thrusts her legs against its steel surface, drives her body into its sloped sides, drops to the bottom and lies quietly, cold, slippery steel curving under her.

She follows the curve, the form of darkness, rises, stretches upward. Steel curves inward overhead. Darkness is all.

She tastes Sony, his wasted particles in the water. Sony, accepting all things, knew no fear.

Something dangles from above, a rope, or a piece of seaweed.

~ ~ ~ ~

Waller, clear headed now, got back in the cab of the tanker, thinking of Mara. It would be terrifying to wake, half drugged, to a blackness such as she had never known. He would get her out as soon as possible.

As he got behind the wheel, one of the boxes tumbled across the gearshift. Shoving it away, his attention was caught by a trivial outdated telephone book. He was sure he had not packed that with his most important books, the logbook and - - -

Wait! Where was the logbook? He dug through the box with both hands. My God! In the rush to pack, he'd picked up the wrong book!

He did not want to deal with Francisco again, did not want to re-enter that insanity, but the logbook was necessary for the girl's future. It was also the record of the only important thing he had ever done in his life. His shovel-torn arm burned with pain as he wrenched the steering wheel, backing and turning the lumbering truck on the narrow road. He must go back.

# 23

~~~~~ REVELATIONS ~~~~~

The last candle wavered and guttered as Francisco examined the water-splotched pages, written in French! How fortunate to be reading the language of his childhood vacations in Paris, rather than English, which he had always resisted and resented. And how revealing, as little by little he recognized Waller's love for the tiny infant he had saved from her dying mother's womb.

Pouring over page after page, he saw Waller's early exultation that at last, he could fulfill his early dream, proving the possibility of a sea based humanity. Trapped into isolation by fear of others, he had moved further and further in the direction of those adaptations he was most familiar with, marine adaptations, until finally, he was unable to reverse them. In the process, the child had become Waller's whole life.

By the time Francisco finished the last pages, he knew that Waller could not bring himself to face the fact that he would never be able to show the world the marvel he had created, even if he made it to Mexico.

With some begrudging sympathy, he saw that Mara had given Waller a reason to live, a way to love in the only way he could, someone totally dependent on him and walled away from the rest of the world.

When he closed the cover of the log, Francisco felt as if he were waking from some strange and exotic dream. He could hear again the lilting song of crickets, smell the honeysuckle, taste salt in the sea air. He felt a bottomless sorrow for the girl, but for the man as well, the tragedy of a brilliant mind so ignorant of life that he did not know a heart will only love when it is free. Love --- the one mystery scientists could never adequately explain.

When the candle sputtered out, he sat in darkness, recalling the near-feverish hysteria of the past days. They had both wanted possession of Mara, and they had nearly killed each other over her. My God.

Still, his anger smoldered. There was no excuse for treating that child like she was not human, throwing her into a tanker like so much fish. What would happen to her now if he made it over the border, as the logbook said he might do?

Francisco prowled the lab, from barred window to barred window, locked door to locked door. He had promised the girl that Waller would never touch her again. Now he had the logbook. He would keep that promise. He would find her and free her, no matter what it took.

Had the man not been so scornful of him, so sure he was a mere peasant, he could have helped him. He knew coastal hideaways in Baja, sheltered coves in the gulf waters. He knew the language of Mexico. And he, Francisco, had taught Mara to trust, something Waller could never do.

The shrill sound of a whirling siren broke into his thinking. The reflection of red lights careened off broken window glass. Grabbing the logbook, he dived under a tarpaulin and lay against the back wall of the lab. They must not find him here.

Waiting, his cheek against concrete, he watched a slug slide across the floor, disappearing in a drain, leaving a trail of slime. A few inches from his face, a tiny pellet like a BB gradually opened up, turning into a sow bug. Water dripped mercilessly loud in the sink nearby. The siren trailed off, and a car door slammed.

Scarcely daring to breathe, he huddled under the smothering green canvas as steps approached and halted at the nearby window. His heartbeat seemed loud enough to give him away. Perhaps some policeman, or even Waller, was already at the window, preparing to unload bullets into the canvas. He heard a man's voice, moving away. "Nobody here, lady. All locked up, power off."

*Lady.* Was Dolores back? Then he heard her voice. "The truck, it is gone." Creeping to the window, Francisco saw her talking to a boyish-looking highway patrolman. "I dunno, my little chickadee. I'm new on the job, mainly handle traffic tickets."

Dolores refused to be taken lightly. "I tell you, I hear shots. I know he is in trouble." She was so close now Francisco could hear her voice tremble. He wanted to call out to her, but then he would be arrested, and in the meantime, the tanker was getting farther away every second. *Get him to leave, Dolores.*

Dolores kept talking. "Officer Shelton, many years Doctor Waller allowed no one on this place. When I come, there are still the secrets, and then came Francisco, *muy intelligente.* He say El Doctor an evil man, and now he is gone too also."

*Get him to leave, Dolores.*

"I never think of myself as specially smart. I am never interest in the confusion clues of murder stories. But now, here I am, right in the muddle of one. The more I try to make it sense, the less sense it is."

Francisco leaned closer, watching. The cop was finally moving toward his squad car. *Let him leave, Dolores.*

She trailed after him, still talking, until he stopped with his hand on the car door. "You told me your boyfriend had been snooping around. That's probably why the Doc took a shot at him. Ever think of that? Sounds like this professor guy just doesn't like people snooping around, that's all." He stooped and picked up a bottle that had slid from Waller's boxes. "A man who loves Scotch and hates people can't be all bad."

*There. He was leaving.*

Dolores kept talking. "Officer, sir. A skull, dead bones, is not funny."

Skull? Bones? Francisco wondered. What bones?

"Lady, he's a scientist. They study old animal bones. We have no right to be snooping around here. If you're afraid to be alone, c'mon, I'll take you to your family. Tomorrow if your boyfriend's not back, you can file a missing person. If he's legal, that is. If he isn't you'll be getting him sent back."

"You wait." Dolores disappeared around the back of the building while the patrolman kicked one shiny boot against the other. She reappeared with a grim-looking skull, clots of mud hanging from long strands of matted black hair. "You see?"

*Cristo.* She had found the body of the mother.

Shelton's voice rose. "Jesus, drop that thing! It means nothing. Doctors study cadavers."

"In high heels? Come, I show you . . ."

"Honey, I'm a highway patrolman, not an anthropologist. I'm just here 'cause you flagged me down. I could get my ass fired, poking around without a warrant." He was getting back in the patrol car.

Francisco clenched his fists in frustration. If Dolores kept this up, Shelton would radio for help, and Waller would be caught. What a mess that would be. Courts, the girl in some institution, and he jailed as accomplice or God knows what. He couldn't stop himself. "Dolores!" he called from the window. "Get me out of here!"

"Francisco!" She raced to the door, rattled the lock. "Are you all right?"

He stuffed the logbook into his daypack, tossed it onto a chair, and pulled one of Waller's old shirts over it.

"Shoot the lock!" Dolores shouted to the patrolman.

"I can't do that. I got no right . . ."

"I see in the movies."

A blast of a revolver, and a moment later Dolores broke into the lab, handing the pistol back to the flustered patrolman.

Sobbing and trembling, she threw her arms around Francisco. "When I find the skull, I so afraid for you."

Holding her, his chin resting on the top of her head, he could feel her heart, beating like a hummingbird's. He felt a sob catch in his own throat that she cared so much for him.

Shelton was taking in the broken glass, the broken chair, the telephone ripped from the wall. "What in the Hell were you doing in here?"

"I am the caretaker. Doctor Waller accidentally locked me in when he left," Francisco said, in his most dignified English.

Shelton looked at his torn shirt, his cuts and bruises. "Only trying to get out. Sure." No way he believed him.

Knowing Waller was traveling farther each second, Francisco could barely conceal his impatience. Standing tall, he looked the other man in the eye. "All right. I work for him. True. But I think he is up to no good, that he keeps someone --- ah---captive in there."

The patrolman took off his billed cap and wiped his forehead. "I gotta say you two got the same imagination. Ought to work for Disney."

Dolores was radiant with pride. "No, Francisco was right all along. El Doctor is... I don't know what he is, but I find that skull buried behind the house."

Francisco didn't like the way this was going. "No, Dolores. You were right, I was wrong. Let this man go on about his business."

Dolores wouldn't quit. "No. Francisco, you were right. Dr. Waller hold someone prisoner in that place." She pushed Shelton toward the domed pool, and he went through the open doors, Dolores right behind him.

Just then Francisco heard the truck laboring up the back road, the sound drifting closer and away, closer and away, on the winding road. There was no mistaking the cranky reluctant cough of that tanker. El Doctor was coming back. Why? What had he done with the girl?

The officer was on the police radio, finally sounding like a cop, all emotion clipped from his voice. "Officer Shelton here. Highway Patrol. Signs of a fight, blood all over the place. Reports somebody kept captive." He repeated Dolores's description of the truck. "If this Waller guy is connected with that body you guys found last week, then he's headed for Mexico. Could be that canyon killer you been lookin' for."

Francisco scooped up the daypack, heavy with the log, and slung it across one shoulder.

Through the trees came the lights of the approaching tanker. Shelton laughed like a nervous Woody Woodpecker. "My second week on the job and I get a real Kookaberra Bird." He started the engine of the squad car. "Quick. Out of sight."

As Shelton hid the car in the trees, Francisco ran for his bicycle.

# 24

~~~~~ APPEARANCES ~~~~~

Waller hadn't slept in more than forty hours. Curves in the road seemed to wriggle like a moving snake as the truck toiled heavily around them. The mystical experience, for that's how he thought of it, stayed with him, more real than the truck, the rutted road, tangible evidence of his existence.

Hands wrenching the steering wheel around curves, he mused about so-called *quantum inter-connectedness.* He'd never had any patience for that kind of thinking. He knew the lingo -- *the bridge between non-local minds, connections to the larger mind, unavailable to us because of the noisy distractions of our ongoing thoughts or our limiting belief systems* -- Whatever. All he knew for sure was what had just happened to him, happened.

The vivid experience of being in the consciousness of other species -- he would remember that always -- it seemed a natural part of him now. *The theory of morphic resonance,* it was called in those papers he'd saved from a quantum physics workshop.

He remembered Dolores's laugh when she first came and he had insisted he wanted to be alone. "No one alone," she said. How much he might have learned from her if he had let himself.

He could now see the dome. In the light of the clouded moon, it seemed once more to crown a grand Spanish resort, the kind of fantasy place where anything could happen. Well, anything certainly had.

Coming around the last bend, he was relieved to see the lab was as he left it, lights out, the place deserted. Francisco had no doubt broken out and taken off. If anybody was coming in response to his telephone call, they would have been here by now.

As he edged the truck into the drive, he thought for a moment he saw the shadowy form of a car back in the trees. Jamming his fingers into the puffy flesh around his eyes, he strained to clear his blurred vision. No. Just nerves. All was quiet, even serene.

He circled and parked the truck headed outward, facing the back road, just in case. Behind the lab he pulled on the power switch. In the glare of outdoor lights, he saw the open lab door, the broken glass, and the bent window bars. Good, he thought, grasping his aching arm. *The son of a bitch is gone.*

In his bedroom, he dug through a cardboard box of papers and found the scientific paper he had been thinking about.

*The Theory of Morphic Resonance: There is some organizing field that transcends space and time, determines the characteristic forms and behavior of living organisms. Once such fields become established through some initial behavior of one organism, that behavior becomes facilitated in others.*

If that's true, Waller thought, then evolution is not accidental. Whether through heredity, cosmic influence, scientific adaptations, or our own spirit, human or animal, we have been willed, or willed ourselves, into what we have become.

Perhaps Mara herself was morphing into a new blend of species, her adaptation to water, her communion with another species, embodied a dramatic change that could facilitate evolutionary change in humans. And more than that, her morphing could even facilitate change in the organizing field - the one mind!

He folded the paper, put it in his pocket, and went to the lab for the logbook. His desk chair lay overturned amidst a scatter of boxes and papers. He jerked open the bottom desk drawer, but it wasn't there. He searched the desk, crates of discarded papers, emptied them on the floor, and stood in the center of chaos. The logbook, the record of all his work, of all Mara's adaptations, was gone. He felt the blood draining from his face.

He was struck, then, by the sight of a muddy skull. He could not at first comprehend what he was seeing. When he realized where it had come from, he dashed to the old irrigation ditch out back. The newly disturbed earth showed traces of torn plastic. Someone had dug up pieces of very old bones. Kneeling, he picked up a shred of crumbling fabric and recognized what was left of the dress the woman had been wearing when he dragged her body out here, so long ago he had almost forgotten. The fabric disintegrated in his fingers.

So -- someone had found her! The car in the shadows then, was posted there to watch him? If so, what were they waiting for?

He edged around to the front of the building and peered out. Sure enough, a squad car, lights out, was easing across the drive and coming to a stop, blocking the exit.

The tanker was some thirty feet away. If he could get to it without being seen there was still a chance for him and the girl. He hesitated. Cops had guns.

Well, everything he'd ever done, even with the best of intentions, had gone awry. Might as well go out in a glaze of gory, as Dolores would say. He headed for the truck.

"Dr. Waller?" Surprisingly hesitant, a young man in uniform approached him, speaking so respectfully, Waller breathed a sigh of relief. Maybe this wasn't as serious as he thought. He put out his hand. "Yes, I'm Dr. Waller."

The patrolman stepped back, obviously repulsed by his filthy lab coat smeared with blood, ragged bandages hanging in dirty tangles from one arm. "Ah ... Officer Shelton here. I just have a few questions, sir."

Just then Waller saw that the tanker hatch was open. He stared, openmouthed. "My God! She must have opened it herself." Had he forgotten she could use her hands? Had he actually begun to think she was a fish? He started for the tanker.

Shelton, reaching for his holster, stopped him. "Okay now. Stay calm. I don't know what's going on here, but let's settle down, nobody's going to hurt you."

Waller pushed past him and scrambled up the tanker's metal ladder, bandages flying. Inside the open hatch, he saw only water. Unbelieving, he bellowed, "She got out!"

Leaping down, ignoring Shelton and his gun, he dropped to his knees to look under the tanker. "Nowhere," he moaned. "She must of got out on the road somewhere! You've got to help me look for her. She may be dying." Tears were coursing down the creases of his face.

Shelton looked at Dolores. She only shrugged, wide-eyed. He tried to keep his gun trained on Waller. "Okay there fella, I don't know who you're talkin' about, but let's get those hands up and then we'll find your little pet whatever."

He fumbled the handcuffs, dropped them, and reached to retrieve them. In that moment, Waller leaped into the cab, the heavy engine roared, and the truck was in motion. As if from under water he heard, "Stop! Don't make me shoot...."

A shot slammed into his side door. He hardly noticed.

Aiming at the rear fender of the patrol car, he gunned the engine. Metal tore against metal and the car swung around like a gate as Waller pushed on through. Another shot shattered the back window.

Throwing on his brights, he drove slowly, searching every shadow, ditch and hollow for a sign of the girl. She knew nothing about vehicles. She might have dropped off the moving truck, fallen under the tires. Anything could have happened.

Farther down the road, just as he was giving up hope, his headlights picked up an unexpected sight. Ahead of him, reflectors whirling madly, was a man on a bicycle. And between his arms on the handlebars a small figure gleamed white in the glare of his headlights. As quickly as it appeared, the vision disappeared around a curve.

The fool Mexican had the girl! All Waller's rage and hopelessness, his weariness, his failure and pain, focused on Francisco. He yelled through the jagged window, "Stop, you idiot!" and reached for the pistol he'd left on the seat. Above the roaring engine and the jolting of the truck, he heard a distant siren. More cops on the way?

Past the horseshoe turn, the pavement had washed out, leaving a narrow ledge easily passable by the bicycle, but not by a fast-moving truck. He hit the brakes; the truck began to swing crazily, careened off the ledge, lunged through brush, and came to a stop against an ancient oak, throwing Waller out.

He lay stunned. Tentatively he moved a leg, an arm, a shoulder. Finally, he pushed himself to his feet and climbed to the road, forgetting his pain.

The bicycle was long gone. "You fool," he yelled into the woods. "She'll die if you keep this up!" The arrogant peasant would not know she would dehydrate if she wasn't back in the water soon.

Shelton's squad car came bumping behind him, the back fender screeching with every rotation of the tire. "C'mon, Dr. Waller. C'mon. Get in."

~ ~ ~ ~

Luckily, Francisco had seen the hatch open, seen her slide out of sight on the other side of the tanker. By the time he got to the girl, she had crawled up under a bush, trembling and terrified, hiding, though anyone could have seen her, so pale and white in the darkness.

He had approached slowly, finger to his lips. She seemed almost too compliant as he lifted her off the ground. Had she been drugged? She let him get her on the handlebars of his bike, clinging to them, balancing as she doubtless balanced on the dolphin's speeding body. He pedaled furiously, keeping his small passenger braced between his arms.

Fortunately, she wasn't fighting him In the darkness it was difficult to avoid ruts, but in a few minutes he heard the truck behind him. Distracted, he rounded a bend too fast, and when his front tire hit a rock, the bicycle careened off the road, throwing him and the girl over the handlebars.

He picked himself up, unhurt, but she lay sprawled in the road. He slung her over his shoulder, a dead weight, and ran for the woods. Dodging dry branches, he scraped through brush, the heavy daypack sliding off his other shoulder.

Behind him, he heard the tanker crash into trees, and the sudden silence. Waller might still pursue him on foot, but for now, he had to find a place to put her down, to make sure she was alright.

In a dark grove of eucalyptus, surrounded by trees and brush, he wrapped her in his denim jacket. Her eyes were open but heavy lidded. She seemed drugged but otherwise unhurt.

He had no idea what to do now. As long as Waller had a gun, it was not the time to try to convince him that he, too, just wanted to keep the girl away from the authorities and get her to a safe place.

He suspected the tanker had gone off the road. He'd heard the crash. He almost hoped Waller had been killed.

Hiding, waiting, he imagined a future, imagined building a grand pool off the coast of Baja, swept clean each day by ocean tides, a grand estate by the Bahia de Los Angeles, like Los Pajaros, with peacocks worked into the wrought iron gates. He and Dolores together could do what Waller couldn't; they would teach the girl to talk and walk. She would never have to be afraid again.

Only a few minutes ago, Dolores was trembling in his arms, so afraid, not for her life, but for his. The memory filled him with deep shame. He had scorned her for fantasies of a woman so flighty she had forgotten him in weeks.

Fantasies faded as he remembered that the logbook said she could be out of water no more than two hours. He ran his hand along her arm. Her tender skin already felt dry as paper. He would have to get her into water soon.

The drugs were evidently wearing off. She pushed herself away from him and sat up, wide-eyed. Her gaze traveled up and up the ragged trunks of eucalyptus and swept across the wide sky, where soft floating clouds revealed, then concealed, brilliant stars one moment, and the next, a glowing half-moon. Her ethereal face, silver in dappled moonlight, reflected quiet awe.

He could only imagine how wondrous the world must seem to her, seeing it for the first time.

The soft night wind carried the scent of brine and a soothing dampness that seemed to refresh her. Grasping a sapling, she stood, teetering on long, tender feet, and sniffed the air. Her rapt gaze turned toward the ocean, out of sight beyond a cleavage of hills.

Her head tilted; she seemed to hear something inaudible to him. Suddenly she lurched forward. Francisco leaped to grab her, but with doubled up legs she kicked out against him and sent him reeling. Focused now and full of purpose, she threw herself down a slope, rolling, crawling, pushing to her feet again, tumbling toward the sea as Francisco lunged to catch her.

Again her powerful legs sent him sprawling, his head striking a limb. He got to his feet, angry now, and tackled her from behind, throwing his weight across her as she fell.

She stared at him, wild-eyed, gasping for air. Francisco got his hands around her waist, grimy with weeds and dirt, and dragged her back up the slope toward the road. Strong, agile as a wild animal, she struggled, her eyes fixed in the direction of the ocean.

Again and again she pushed free and scrambled away, fell, and pulled herself up, until finally, he thought she would stay where she fell. Stepping back, he let her lay. He watched in pity as this dolphin girl, so graceful and light in water, so crippled on land, got up, teetered for a step or two, then pitched forward again, crawling away with new lacerations, as terrified of him now as she had been of Waller.

"Don't run," he said, gentle now. "Please. I only want to help you."

She cowered away, scrambling on hands and knees into a thicket, cowering there as clouds covered the moon.

He crawled through the brush after her, but she was lost in darkness. Blindly he groped out of the thicket, branches lashing at his face, brittle broken twigs cutting his hands. When he crawled out the other side and stood in a clearing, she was nowhere in sight. He listened. Not a sound. It seemed hopeless.

He had seen the look, the longing, the fierce vitality that came over her when she faced the ocean, when the wind carried its scent. Had she heard, perhaps, the call of dolphins?

He had to find her. She was no dolphin. She could not live in that violent sea, its pounding waves, its jagged rocks.

The cloud cover broke for a moment, and he plunged through the trees toward the sea. He had to find her.

# 25

Mara hides under prickly brush in the darkest part of the woods, fearing her breathing will give her away. She claps a hand over her mouth when she feels Francisco's footfalls passing, then moving away.

She lies still long after he is gone. Outside brings terrors she has never known -- trapped in hard steel blackness, moving water slapping her this way and that. Finally pulling herself up on a dangling rope, climbing out through the sky circle, only to slide down hard steel and fall onto hard ground.

Worse, the Francisco who scooped her up and put her on a wheeled ride is not the gentle creature who sings and brings sweet things to eat. Maybe there are two Franciscos. Maybe when the land beings are not around water, they change, like she does when she sleeps in the sun too long and her shrinking skin makes her frantic.

When she is sure he is gone, she crawls from the brush and sits up. Gradually her trembling stops. Peering through twisted black branches, she can make out the pale outline of the dome, far, far, away that safe secure place where she was cared for. And way, way above that, there is another dome, a much, much bigger dome, pricked with many tiny holes where bright light twinkles and a round globe glows and disappears in cloudy vapor.

Alone in this limitless and terrifying Outside, she remembers the safety of her pool, the sure and secure sameness of her daily existence. She remembers Sony's anguished cries as Waller drags him from the water.

In the woods, quiet now, she hears Sony calling -- a distant call but certain. She has been hearing him for days, a hollow dreamlike signal, steady and patient and calm, as if it were only a matter of time. She dare not answer him now, with Francisco near, but she knows he is close, and she must follow.

Ignoring the pain of rocks and branches tearing at her tender feet, she throws herself forward, letting his signals direct her.

The invigorating scent of salty brine comes again on the night breeze and she feels a welcome dampness in the air as she makes her way downhill.

Suddenly she trips, falls, trapped in something she cannot see, something that sends darts through her skin each time she moves, tears her skin then wraps even tighter. She cannot move without pain. With one bleeding hand she pushes against the wires that spiral around her, wires embedded with sharp barbs. The more she struggles, the more they tighten.

She can only lie still, helpless, dry skin prickling with dirt and grass, head throbbing.

Sony calls. She twists and struggles. Let the darts tear her skin, make them release her from their tightening grip. Sony calls.

~ ~ ~ ~

Dolores saw Francisco take off on his bike with something --- or someone --- on the handlebars. Then Waller crashed the big water truck into the cop's car, and the truck roared after the bicycle, a lumbering elephant after a mosquito.

While Officer Shelton pried at his crunched fender, she slipped through the fence where the gray horse was pastured.

He stretched out his long neck, large soulful eyes eager for treats. "Sorry, Caballo," she said, holding out empty hands, "No apples this time." The horse lowered its big head and nuzzled her palms, groping with large soft lips. Getting a hold on his halter, she led him to her mounting stump and pulled herself onto his broad, solid back.

Guiding Caballo with the firm grip of her knees and gentle tugs on his mane, she let him pick his way through the woods, the shortcut to the beach. The moon had disappeared again, but the horse knew the way.

She did not know where Francisco was, or where he was going. She only knew the back road led to the beach.

Caballo trotted slowly, and she hadn't gone far when from the road came the sound of a crash. Pulling back on the halter, she listened. Quiet. Waller could not drive that fast on the back road. No one could. She hoped he was all right. Well, at least no fighting, no guns, no sirens.

She gave Caballo a nudge with her heel, and moved on. The clouds had gathered and a fine rain was blowing in from the ocean.

That would make it hard for Francisco, a bike on a muddy road. She urged Caballo onward, looking for a break in the trees where she might see the road.

About a mile down the path, as they passed rotting fence posts and tangled wire, the horse spooked, jerking his head up, dancing sideways, eyes rolling.

Calming him to a standstill, she saw something caught in a coil of barbed wire, and slid down off his back. Nearby lay a pale, childlike creature, the figure she'd seen on Francisco's bicycle, motionless as a trapped rabbit. So this was the secret Dr. Waller kept in the domed pool. This was Francisco's secret. This was what she'd been so upset about?

She knelt, speaking to it softly, as if she were soothing a wild animal. In the darkness, she could make out long webbed fingers, a white hairless head. The girl --- for this was a girl, though a strange one --- was motionless. Dolores was sure the creature was breathing, thank goodness, taking in long, deep breaths.

"It's all right, little one," she murmured. "I will help you." Calmly murmuring, she carefully lifted loops of barbed wire off bare skin, skin that felt unlike anything she had ever touched, more like dry chamois than skin. It was badly torn and bleeding, and dirty and cracked in places, as if it had baked dry before the rain came. The hair on the child's head was short and downy, reminding her of a cousin's new baby.

She had to keep pushing her own wet hair back from her face as she patiently worked to untangle the barbed wire without hurting the child, who only lay still as a frightened animal.

As the rain fell harder, she felt the girl's skin change from dry, cracked leather to something more like damp rose petals. She seemed to come to life with the rain. Dolores lay a gentle hand on her shoulder to keep her from moving. "Hold still. We're almost done," she murmured, carefully unwinding the last of the wire. The child seemed to understand, for she quieted again.

Once free, though, she shied away, staring at Dolores from wild eyes deep in the hollows of her unworldly face.

"I won't hurt you," Dolores said, holding out her wide-open hands. For long minutes they studied each other, each as though they had never seen a creature quite like the other before. For a long while there was only the sound of the diminishing shower, and rain dropping gently off leaves.

Staring into her eyes, the child reached out a long webbed hand and pressed the palm to the side of Dolores's wet face. Gradually, her wide eyes changed from fear to wonder. Dolores scarcely breathed for fear of breaking the sacred moment.

Impulsively, she put her own hand on the creature's cheek, wet with rain, and held it there in rapt amazement. She felt the great rush of blood and energy that was a living thing, a great waterfall, pulsing through a beating heart. The moment seemed to encompass her and all living things.

She felt the great humming of the child's heart in harmony with her own. She knew she was tuning in to a consciousness different from her own, or maybe deeper than her own.

The world curved around them somehow, and she felt, rather than saw, all the small creatures living in the trees and heard those scurrying beneath the ground. She knew more than ever before what her grandmother really meant when she said, "We are all a part of God."

To her mind came visions of washing waves and dancing kelp, dolphins weaving and jumping in play. She felt the longing in this angelic creature, a primitive force, like her own longings multiplied a thousand times.

Tears welled up in the other's luminous, gentle eyes, and she felt her own tears. The girl smiled, a flat lipless smile, showing no teeth. Dolores felt the smile on her own full lips.

A twig snapped and suddenly Francisco was there. "Thank God you found her, Dolores. She is quick as a deer."

The girl looked about wildly, tried to bolt past him, but he threw himself on her, bringing her down hard, one arm around her neck as she bucked like a calf.

"Francisco! Stop!" Dolores cried.

The girl's head came up, deliberate and hard, hit him a sharp blow on the chin, and she scrambled loose.

Furious now, he picked up a stone.

"Francisco!" Dolores stared in horror, seeing the man in her dream, the man with the rock in his hand.

Francisco looked at the stone as if he had never seen it before and dropped it, but he held on to the girl. "If we let her go, Dolores, she will head right for the ocean." He thought of sharks, of stingrays. He thought of logs pounded to shreds against the rocks. How could she possibly survive out there?

"Francisco, look at her. It's what she wants."

"How can she know what she wants? She's never been free."

Dolores knelt, stroking the trembling shoulders. "She knows. You mus' listen to her." She took his hand and held it against the girl's face. "You can feel it, no? You can see as she sees?"

She watched Francisco's face. Did he have heart enough, was it open enough, to receive? The desperate anger was gone, but his face clouded with a dark surge of fear, and she knew it was fear that kept him from receiving.

When he let go of the girl's arm, Dolores grabbed her by the waist and threw her onto the back of the horse.

"Dolores! No! You'll send her to her death!"

To her amazement, the girl seemed entirely at home there, clinging to the mane, wrapping her long legs around the flanks of Caballo, who backed and pranced in response to her pressing knees, her gentle kicks.

Francisco stood in the middle of the trail, blocking the path to the sea.

The girl leaned into the neck of the horse, making the clicking sounds Dolores had often heard coming from the pool. The horse danced in a circle, backed a few feet, and ran directly at Francisco. He reared, hooves high over their heads. Francisco hit the ground fast. As though carried by his rider's will, the huge beast soared over him and galloped away.

Francisco scrambled to his feet, furious. "Do you know what you've done?"

Dolores took his hands and looked into his eyes. "Francisco, she is more than you think her to be. She knows what she wants."

He stared after the galloping horse. "My God. She rides him like she rode the dolphin!"

The headlights of a car filtered through the trees above them, followed by the scrape and clank of Shelton's damaged patrol car. "Quick! We've got to flag them down." Grabbing her hand, he started through the brush toward the road. "If we catch them, we can cut her off at the coast."

~ ~ ~ ~

## 26

~~~~~ **MUERTE O LA MER** ~~~~~

Mara laughs with exhilaration. The easy rise and fall of the galloping animal is like Sony's rhythmic plunges, rushing her through rain-swept air the way Sony sped through water, her body one with his. All he needs to urge him on is a touch from her hands, the hard clutch of her knees, her clicks and trills. Somewhere ahead, Sony is calling, calling.

In the froth of her mind still lives the image of the beautiful land-being who freed her from the painful trap, a creature very much like herself, with a voice soft as music and hands that heal. A land-being who receives. She has not known that oneness since Sony.

Sony is calling.

The horse breaks from the woods into a clearing and she is flying across the curvature of the world, seeing before her a great shimmering expanse of moving water. She throws back her head and warbles an answer to Sony's signals. *I am coming.*

Joy rises in her, the joy of a world huge and without limits. Clinging to Caballo's mane, she lets the joy flow through her, into the waiting night.

Somewhere below, where sea and rainy air meet, is Sony, now so near. She presses her knees into the flanks of the horse and he leaps forward. Her own voice spirals joyously into the great freedom of the ocean before her.

~ ~ ~ ~

Officer Shelton drove the crippled patrol car, one flat tire thudding the ground and scraping the fender, through the light rain, Waller in the passenger seat, fussing, shaking his head as he scanned the woods on each side of the road, repeating and repeating, "I've got to find her. She could die out here."

"Hey. You can find her, whatever she is, with my spotlight if you want."

"You have to slow down." Waller said, querelous.

"Slow as you want," the patrolman said. "Can't go much faster with that fender bashed in anyways." He reached for the spotlight and showed him how to operate it.

As they limped along, Waller swept the light across every inch of the roadsides. "Thank God for the rain squall, or her skin would have cracked long ago."

"What is this *she* anyway, a turtle? An alligator?"

Waller ignored him. The spotlight revealed nothing except brush, trees, and an occasional washed out dirt bank. "God only knows where she is by now," he agonized.

When Shelton maneuvered the squad car around another curve, the headlights fell on Francisco, flagging him down, the woman behind him, hugging herself against the rain.

"Don't stop for that idiot!" Waller roared.

"C'mon," Shelton laughed, stopping the car. "Be nice."

"Could have killed her," Waller muttered.

As Francisco climbed into the back seat, Waller twisted around, reaching for him. "Whatn'hell did you think you were doing? Where is she?"

"Hey!" Shelton ordered. "Settle down, old man!" Dolores got in back with Francisco, but Shelton waited to go on until Waller settled back in his seat.

While Francisco urged him to hurry and Waller kept asking him to slow down, Shelton maneuvered the car carefully around the last mile to the old beachfront road. Coming from the highway, the sheriff's deputies had gotten there first. Two squad cars were already positioned on the parking lot and four officers were unloading rifles while another focused a spotlight on the ragged cliff descending to the beach.

Even before Shelton brought it to a halt by the old hotdog stand, Francisco and Dolores jumped from the car and ran up the slope toward the dark line of trees where the woods ended at a broad open hillside. Waller watched, hand on the door handle.

Turning off the engine, Shelton looked at Waller's shaggy white head, his bloodied lab coat, his tormented, blood-shot eyes, wondering what to do with him. Who was he? Just an isolated old eccentric doing experiments the hired help didn't understand? A famous scientist doing top-secret work? Or a dangerous nutcase who should be cuffed? "While we're waiting for things to settle down, Dr. Waller, how about some I.D.?"

Waller fished a slim, battered wallet out of a back pocket.

"Want to tell me what's going on?" Shelton asked, while he studied faded documents. "Drivers license hasn't been renewed in years," he noted. "Lucky I didn't catch you driving." He laughed, slightly embarrassed. The documents showed the man was *Doctor* Al Waller, all right, with impressive credentials.

"So there's a woman buried in your back yard, Dr. Waller. Know anything about that?"

Peering out the windshield like a hound sensing a rabbit, Waller didn't answer. Shelton slipped a cuff around one wrist. "I'm kind of in over my head here, Doctor Waller. Not going to sue me, are you? Huh?" He laughed his Woody Woodpecker laugh.

Waller waved his free hand in the direction of Dolores and Francisco, disappearing into the darkness on top of the hill. "They must know where she is . . ."

"They don't seem dangerous," Shelton said. "Maybe they just want to help you find her. Who is she, anyway?"

Silence.

"Well okay," Shelton said agreeably, "Waiting for a lawyer. Right?" He glanced nervously at the luminous hands of his watch. Should have been home long ago, his wife would be worried. "Sir, I'm going to have to turn you over to the sheriff. I'm just the Highway Control --- now I'm talking like Dolores --- I mean Highway Patrol." He laughed nervously. "Hate to do it, but..." He reached for Waller's arm.

Waller threw himself out of the car, and was already heading up the hill ... with a gun in his hand. *Wheren'hell did he get that? My ass is fried.*

Francisco reached the top of the slope just as the horse came galloping out of the woods, the girl urging it on, heading for the sea. He couldn't let that happen.

Throwing himself directly in the path of the horse, he waved his arms. Wild-eyed, the huge beast reared and whirled, sending the girl spinning. He watched in horror as she fell. The animal thundered away, and she lay on the grassy slope, dazed and struggling to get up.

A searchlight was slowly combing the hill. Though she fiercely resisted, he got her up off the ground and half-carried, half-dragged her, back toward the shadowed woods, and gently laid her in a shallow, shadowed depression. Hoping she might understand the words, he said, "If we stay down, the light will pass over our heads." Squirming from his grasp, she pushed to her feet. For just one moment, her shining white form stood out in the brilliant light.

Someone shouted, "Look! That a woman up there?" The light circled back toward them.

Francisco pulled her down. Terrified, the girl struggled, but finally lay next to him, trembling.

Dolores stepped into the place where the girl had stood, stepped directly into the sweeping searchlight, shouting and waving her arms. "It is only me, Dolores. I look for my husband."

Decoying the light away from the girl, she walked toward the men below.

~ ~ ~ ~

Stopping on the top of the embankment to catch his labored breath, Waller saw Dolores in the bright spotlight. And Mara too? He thought he had seen her atop the horse, small and white against the dark trees, but the horse had galloped away without a rider.

White trunks of eucalyptus, stripped like bones, threw barred shadows in scattered patterns across the slope. He thought he could make out a dark figure hunched close to the ground. Grateful that the greenhorn cop had not searched under his lab coat, he held the gun steady and crept toward Francisco.

Below, another squad car came careening around the bend, wailing siren cutting the air like a lariat. Car doors slammed, and Waller paused long enough to see two more men tear rifles off a rack. He heard Shelton shouting, "First thing I knew he was charging that hill like Teddy Roosevelt."

Coming up quietly from behind, Waller stood over Francisco and the girl. "Idiot! Let her go!" He fired a warning shot into the ground.

The girl, paralyzed with fear, curled into herself, hiding her eyes, covering her ears with her palms.

As Francisco leaped up, threatening to attack, Waller aimed, fired again, and Francisco's leg doubled under him. He held his hands up as if they could stop more bullets. "Don't shoot, Doctor Waller," he said in French. "*Ne tire pas.* I know now what you have tried to do. I can help you. *Assister.*"

French! The man spoke French! Amazed, Waller lowered the gun.

Francisco spoke hurriedly, still in French. "You gave her life. If she is to live, you are the only one who can say. We must work together."

Waller stepped toward the trembling child, her delicate skin torn and bleeding. "Mara." She drew back, about to bolt, eyes wide in their dark hollows.

Shouts erupted from below. Running feet. The spotlight circled toward them. Waller looked down the hill at the policemen with their uniforms and their rifles. No use thinking of Mexico.

For long seconds he looked toward the ocean. The smell of the sea was strong in the wet salty air, bringing with it images from his recent trance --- the powerful yearning, the beckoning of the sea. "*La Mer*," he told Francisco. "You must get her to the sea. It is her only hope."

Turning, he deliberately walked into the glaring light, his white lab coat dazzling. The spotlight held him like a man on stage, long tangled hair like white flame around his head, the gun at a crazy angle in his outstretched hand.

He could see nothing but a great ring, a ring of white light, golden and rainbow hued around the edges. The hollow, distorted sound of a loudspeaker loomed like the voice of a young and insecure God. "Dr. Waller, please! Stop where you are!"

One arm lifted to shield his eyes, Waller fired directly into the center of the spotlight. Sudden darkness. Then an explosion of rifle fire.

~ ~ ~ ~

Mara is shaken to her very bones. As she sees his blood seep in black rivulets down the side of his lab coat, she feels her own blood thinning. "Whar," she warbles softly. "Whar."

She pushes against Francisco's restraining arms, leans toward the terrible sight, sees already his colors dissipating, dimming. Soon, she knows he will be just an empty shell, a hollow husk. "Whar."

~ ~ ~ ~

Dolores watched the two officers standing over Waller, their rifle barrels pointed at him, like boys poking sticks at a snake. Tears streaming, she watched El Doctor's unmoving bulk. A steadily widening stain blossomed on the front of his white lab coat, slightly to the left.

Evidently satisfied that he was dead, they searched the darkness. "Whatnhell was he shooting at?" Seeing nothing, they started downhill, their voices softening, caught in the awe and power of death. "Well, guess we got our man, crazy old coot."

~ ~ ~ ~

Francisco looked out across the ocean, hearing Waller's last words -- *Get her to the sea. It is her only hope.* -- *La mer, el mar ... Muerte o La Mer*, death or the sea. Such small distinctions had kept them apart. And now, the girl . . .

The Pacific Ocean stretched forever, mirroring the path of a shrouded moon. Waves pounded the rocks, tearing at the shore. Inexplicably, he remembered an old French song. *The bells of St. Mary's, ah, hear they are calling ...*

~ ~ ~ ~

Mara understands Francisco is not the mad animal now. Maybe the rain has loosened the tightness of his skull, maybe something else she does not understand, but the craziness is over. The terrifying sirens, the men with guns, they are fading into darkness, fading into distance.

She is not afraid of this Francisco, the one with the soft voice, the gentle touch. She lets him get his shoulder under her and lift her to her feet, though she can feel in her own body the pain of his bullet-smashed leg.

Without fear, her thinking clears. All she is aware of now is the gleaming ocean and the call of dolphins. She knows there are many of them, Sony and many other Sonys. She hears their calls like distant music, all singing at once, like something ancient she dimly recalls. Closer to shore, Sony signals, *Come. Come. Come.*

With Francisco's help, she stands facing Sony's world of water, enraptured as the emerging white moon tinges the rolling whitecaps with silver.

Francisco's supporting arm is neither holding her back, or forcing her forward. She knows he is waiting for her to show him what she wants, even though she feels his fear in the stiffness of his hard muscles. She takes a step forward.

Leaning into each other like some two-headed four-legged creature, Francisco helps Mara to the steep embankment, then they slide, roll and tumble to the bottom. Lying in the damp sand, he holds the girl against him, feeling the rapid beat of her heart against his chest. His own heart beats faster in fear for her. A rock has ripped his backpack open and the logbook lies a few feet away. Waves lap at their feet

Ignoring the pain in his injured leg, he pushes himself up with the other. Mara stands on her own, enthralled, focused on the sea. He thinks perhaps she sees the flash of dolphins, hears their ultrasonic cry, far out across the water.

He reaches out, aching to hold onto her, sees Dolores hurrying toward them, withdraws his hand.

Teetering on arched, finned feet, Mara faces the sea, her face shining with wonder. Her nostrils flare. Her throat pulses, gill-like scars shine in the moonlight. Her entire body trembles.

Between her and freedom lies a jagged rock. Francisco stoops, picks up Waller's logbook, opens the wet, ink-smeared pages, and puts it face down across the rock's knife-like edges. Mara takes one step, hesitates on the book's protective surface, plunges into the sea, and is gone.

The next wave curls up and around the book, lifts it high, then it too disappears, leaving only a few tiny hermit crabs scrambling about on the sand.

~ ~ ~ ~

~ ~ ~ ~

~ ~ ~ ~

# ~~~~~ *EPILOGUE* ~~~~~

The papers were full of morgue shots of El Professor, grim-looking in death. The face of a true madman, one caption said. There was much speculation about how many other bodies would be found at the old laboratory. There were sinister pictures of the octopus.

The report that someone had spotted a mysterious female figure on the night of Waller's death caused more speculation. One tabloid, with lurid, retouched photos, said it was a futuristic human, come up from the sea. Another said it was a throwback, descendent of those who had, eons ago, remained on land rather than return to the sea with their kind. When anyone asked Dolores, and few did, she only said, "*Quien Sabe?* Who knows?"

Across the border, the Mexican press had different stories. One marine biologist, formerly taken seriously, said she may have been a human/dolphin adaptation, once known to exist somewhere in the San Diego area. When Waller's will was found, Dolores and Francisco became partners in restoring the lab to its original use. By the time they had their second child, *Los Pajaros* had become the most popular resort in the region.

Waller's grave was now a tourist site, and Dolores planted roses there. When Francisco watched her tenderly tamping dirt over the roots, a smudge over one lovely cheek, his heart ached with pleasure. He didn't understand how he could not have loved her all along.

Each night at sundown, they biked to the cove and walked along the shore. Sometimes they saw dolphins leaping and frolicking in the waves. Sometimes, far out on the dazzling sea, they thought they saw Sony, leaping toward the sky, and on his back, the silver figure of a girl. Just a glimpse, and they were gone.

~ ~ ~ ~

~ ~ ~ ~

~ ~ ~ ~

# ACKNOWLEDGMENTS

*Thanks first to John Lilly's scientific work: <u>Lilly on Dolphins; humans of the sea,</u> which inspired my interest in dolphins. Thanks go to my patient family, who tentatively have faith in me while I live in my writing world. Thanks to my friends, Nanci Woody and Clysta Kinstler, and all the others who read the first version years ago, and encouraged me to finish it. Thanks to my writing group, Antoinette May, Kevin Arnold, and Lucy Sanna, published authors all, who added their professional expertise. Thanks to Charles Herndon, who saw that little Mara needed to be heard as well as seen. She now has her own point of view. I only wish the dolphins could give us theirs. Finally, my gratitude to my readers.*

*Helen Bonner, 2011*

Dr. Helen Bonner, formerly a Professor of English at Minnesota State University, has a PhD in Communications, Creative Writing and Screen Writing. While still an undergraduate, she won the best screenplay award at Ohio University with A Higher Loyalty: The Jeannette Rankin Story, optioned in L.A. Her short stories have been published widely, and her plays produced in local theaters. Her memoir, Laid Daughter, is being used in cultural trauma classes, and a later memoir, First Love Last, is a book club favorite. Her novel, Cry Dance, about clashing cultures, is being read in Literature courses. In her Northern California home, she is working on a novel of the '70's, MsDemeanors.

## A Conversation with Helen Bonner

Q.   Your previous books were memoirs, therefore realistic. Even the Novel, Cry Dance, is not beyond possibility. What was on your mind when you started The Dolphin Papers, Sci-fi bordering on fantasy?

HB.  Great question but difficult to answer. I had just read Lily's great book on Dolphins. An animal lover, I was horrified that dolphins were being used to carry explosives and blown up along with their targets, and fascinated that they had once been land animals, like us. I also knew that newborn babies can swim. Stirring those together, my imagination came up with Dr. Waller, who tries to wall himself off from humans, but can relate to animals. After that, the story seemed to shape itself along the lines of *Frankenstein*, though Mara is no monster.

Q.   Two Hispanics got stirred into that mix. How come?

HB.  I'm interested in the ways we separate ourselves from others, make ourselves "different." Language is one of the ways. Only when Waller quits walling himself off from Francisco does he know who he really is. What separates Francisco from Dolores, however, are ideas like upper and lower class.

Q.   Why all the talk about evolution?

HB.  Like Waller, I believe that the process of evolution doesn't just stop with us. It is still going on. The fact that dolphins were once land animals, like us, makes me wonder what might be our next evolutionary step? Why did dolphins return to the ocean? If we run out of earth's resources, or create a war-torn or polluted earth, might we someday have to do the same?

Q.   Why do you write?

HB.  Why do birds sing? Probably in the genes. My father and my son are story tellers. Writing gives me a way to express possibilities in a way that people enjoy. Entertaining stories slip ideas in the back door, so to speak.

## *Discussion topics for book groups:*

A. Dr. Waller is not the conventional protagonist or antagonist, hero or villain. In what ways is he a good man? In what ways might he be considered evil? What is your definition of evil?

B. How do Waller's habits feed into the dilemma he finds himself in? Consider for example; drinking too much, avoiding people, judging them harshly, or procrastinating.

C. Does Waller have an obligation to save the unborn baby? Does he give his life, in effect, to save her? If so, is he then heroic? Has he redeemed himself?

D. Waller is studying dolphin communication. Are dolphins in this novel better at communicating than humans?

E. Do you think it is possible that some animals in some ways might be smarter than humans? For example?

F.  Two men are fighting to control the life of a seven-year-old girl. Dolores says the child knows what she wants, and frees her to make her own choice. Do you think she did the right thing?

G.  Some cultures, or some men, deny women control of their own lives by "protecting" them. In that way, could Mara be seen as symbolic or her story a parable?

MAY 0 5 2012

CPSIA information can be obtained at www.ICGtesting.com
Printed in the USA
BVOW011510260911

272070BV00001B/4/P